Rags
A Shaker Love Story

by
Joseph Durante and Louis Durante

iUniverse, Inc.
Bloomington

Rags
A Shaker Love Story

Copyright © 2012 by Joseph Durante and Louis Durante

All rights reserved. No part of this book may be used or reproduced by any means, graphic, electronic, or mechanical, including photocopying, recording, taping or by any information storage retrieval system without the written permission of the publisher except in the case of brief quotations embodied in critical articles and reviews.

This is a work of fiction. All of the characters, names, incidents, organizations, and dialogue in this novel are either the products of the author's imagination or are used fictitiously.

iUniverse books may be ordered through booksellers or by contacting:

iUniverse
1663 Liberty Drive
Bloomington, IN 47403
www.iuniverse.com
1-800-Authors (1-800-288-4677)

Because of the dynamic nature of the Internet, any web addresses or links contained in this book may have changed since publication and may no longer be valid. The views expressed in this work are solely those of the author and do not necessarily reflect the views of the publisher, and the publisher hereby disclaims any responsibility for them.

Any people depicted in stock imagery provided by Thinkstock are models, and such images are being used for illustrative purposes only.

Certain stock imagery © Thinkstock.

ISBN: 978-1-4697-0051-9 (sc)
ISBN: 978-1-4697-0053-3 (hc)
ISBN: 978-1-4697-0052-6 (e)

Library of Congress Control Number: 2012910519

Printed in the United States of America

iUniverse rev. date: 5/31/2012

Dedicated to Lorraine Durante,

wife and mother.

Special thanks to Rose McCoy.

Contents

The Story ix
About the People and the Times xi
Main Characters xiii

Chapter 1	The Storm	1
Chapter 2	The Story Begins	3
Chapter 3	Inside the House	6
Chapter 4	The Doctor's Visit	15
Chapter 5	Ain't Scared	22
Chapter 6	Yard Work	25
Chapter 7	In Our Prayers	31
Chapter 8	The Shaker Village	35
Chapter 9	Planting Corn	45
Chapter 10	Gathering the Ice	52
Chapter 11	The Good Room	56
Chapter 12	The First Block	58
Chapter 13	The First Loaf of Bread	60
Chapter 14	Returning Home	61
Chapter 15	The Tree	63
Chapter 16	Christmas Church	65
Chapter 17	The General Store	67
Chapter 18	Apple Picking	71
Chapter 19	The Church	73
Chapter 20	The Mouse	79
Chapter 21	A New Morning	82
Chapter 22	A Quiet Afternoon on the Lake	84

Chapter 23	A New Life	88
Chapter 24	Our Hero Rags	98
Chapter 25	The Barber Shop	102
Chapter 26	The J.J. Jenkins Train and Brake Shoe Factory	106
Chapter 27	The Invitation. Rags Tells His Family History	110
Chapter 28	The Promise	130
Chapter 29	Stretch and Noaccount	133
Chapter 30	A Little Older	141
Chapter 31	Sophia	144
Chapter 32	The Aunt	154
Chapter 33	The Institution	163
Chapter 34	Barber Shop News	164
Chapter 35	Hooch	166
Chapter 36	Rags Visits Billy	168
Chapter 37	Cow Tipping	172
Chapter 38	The Trial	174
AUTHORS MESSAGE		179
ABOUT THE AUTHOR		181

The Story

Our story which transgresses several generations has its origin, its roots as it were in Shaker country at the Shaker community in Hancock, Massachusetts. It is a two part story that runs side by side interrelating the older more disciplined life of grandfather Joshua with the more carefree and modern life of his grandson Rags. The story contrasts the similarities of living in a different time. The mix of hardship and comedy is referenced by running the two parts of the story together integrating them as the story of Rags and Patches develops.

The story opens in hardship as the young boy Joshua a victim of life's tragedy is left orphaned. For a short time he is taken in and cared for by strangers but later is delivered to the people at the Shaker village to be raised. In a time when there were no orphanages the community provided ideal refuge. It is here that we see Joshua grow and learn the ways of the Shaker people. As Joshua matures into a young man he falls in love with Sara. The inner conflict of their feelings and the Shaker dogma of celibacy results in Joshua leaving the community, and taking Sara with him who he takes to wife. After leaving the village the two start a new way of life. The enterprising Joshua builds a fine foundation for himself and his family only to have tragedy take their only son from them. Their son had a child and as fate would have it Joshua and Sara are left to raise their only grandson, whose name is Rags. Rags, although having inherited the abilities of his heritage, is different from his grandfather Joshua in many ways. However, as our story develops and unbeknown to Rags he too will have to one day raise a son, a young boy named Patches who has adopted Rags as his family.

This story is a parallel of hard times and good times, of more simple times and more complex times. It is a contrast and a parallel in work ethic and brings us back to a way of life in the hard but fun filled "good old days".

About the People and the Times

<u>The Shakers of the 1800's</u> : This unique and fascinating people once prospered among mountains ablaze with autumn color in the heart of the beautiful Massachusetts Berkshires. There in the village of Hancock which was nestled with all of its neatness and order in the bosom of endless natural wonder lived an extraordinary group of people called the Shakers. This fascinating people had the uncanny knack of finding the most functional way of doing anything. Simplicity and perfection was the earmark of the Shaker way of life. Perhaps they are best known to this day for their flawless furniture with its beautiful, simple and classic lines. However, the packaging of seeds for sale, the invention of the circular saw and of pipe making machinery, the side hill plow, clothes pins and the flat broom as well as improvements made in the perfection of the automatic washing machine and printing press are just some examples of accomplishments that give testimony to the extent of their inventiveness and ingenuity. The list of accomplishments that attest to the Shaker ability seems endless. To add just a few, there was the seed planting machine, the metal pointed pen, and the round stone barn.

In spite of their industrial abilities they were in actuality an agricultural communal society growing most of what they needed to survive. On their beautiful farms they grew many varieties of crops, fruit trees and herbs.

The Shakers were a peace loving people professing great faith and manifesting within themselves a certain and obvious inner peace and calm for all to see. Although they did not allow themselves to focus on things of this world they did however indeed prosper.

There was much singing and dancing associated with the religious service of the Shaker people. In fact it was the dancing during the service that led to their name, the "Shaking Quakers". It was a unique marching type of dance during the service which would often find them worked to a frenzy, for it was during this dance ceremony so unique to this group that they would shake off sin and gather in blessings. During this peculiar marching type dance it was believed that the Shakers that were already gone to Heaven would shower down blessings upon those still here. And so as part of this dance they would motion with both their arms and hands as if taking in blessings from above.

Because of their dogma of celibacy it was not uncommon to find orphans and converts among the membership. In fact the growth of the membership was to a great extent dependent upon converts and unbelievers who became believers.

The Shakers were a people with a work ethic of excellence, in which all work must be done equally well, free from error and fancy design.

Neatness and an attitude of excellence in the production of quality goods, while living in an atmosphere of peace, was what the Shakers were all about.

Main Characters

Joshua: Grandfather Joshua Jenkins, old J.J., is the grandfather of our hero. As an orphan he once belonged to the family community of Shakers at Hancock. But old Josh when he was young fell in love with Sara. Determined not to be vanished as the sect eventually was by its own rule of celibacy, Joshua leaves the shadow of Mt. Greylock bringing with him a new wife Sara and the industrious nature of his upbringing. Then in a not too distant town the young Josh starts the local brake shoe factory which for the generations of our story supported nearly all of the townspeople. The "J.J. Jenkins Train and Brake Shoe Factory" is located alongside the railroad tracks at the end of town.

Sara: The one other thing that Joshua brought out of Hancock with him was Sara. Together they will build a life that is touched by both bliss and catastrophe. Sara nicknames her son Isaac, "Rags." Isaac is killed by a catastrophic fire at the factory. Anna, his wife, dies leaving their only boy child to be raised by Sara and Joshua. Sara names her new grandson "Rags" after his dad.

Rags: The grandson of old J.J. and Sara who becomes a sultry old buster whose inheritance allows him to do exactly what he wanted to do in life....nothing. He is actually a rich pauper a little too respectable to be called a bum, with only a fine line and considerable money separating truth from reality. Rags is in complete control of his own destiny. He is a boisterous, bold and crass man content to float on the tides of life moving from occasion to occasion like a full grown cigar smoking baby being rocked in the arms of time. With the attitude of not spoiling his young and healthy life with work he is content to enjoy the younger years, saving the later for what work might have to be done, but with all due respect, never really intending that such an event might actually occur. Yet with all this, when the sun shown each day the very first thing that it would light up was Rags' face which always seemed to show like a summer Santa Clause full of energy and magic. He needed nothing, but had everything. Life was serving him. His heritage of simplicity could easily be seen in his dress and attitude, but his heritage of perfection…lost, completely lost, somehow, somewhere along the way.

Little did Rags know that soon a boy would enter into his private domain changing the meaning of life for him. He loved the simple life and best of all it seemed he loved playing the role of a pauper. He…Rags… who everyone in town considered to be the town pauper and least important among them was in fact the heir and owner of the brake shoe factory upon which almost the entire town in one way or another was dependent. He was the grandson of old J.J. but no one knew it with the exception of old Doc Jones and Sophia. Doc had passed on many, many years ago and ole' Sophia, well she just never told anyone anything. And so for now Rags was content to oversee his world from a park bench. But all of this would soon change. Why? …Because of a little boy called Patches.

<u>Billy</u>: Billy, who Rags names Patches, is the little freckled faced boy who grows up during our story under the tutorship of Rags. We watch Patches grow from a boy running with his dog in the streets of an unknown town in Massachusetts into a self-taught,

hardworking young man made wise in the ways of the world by one most unlikely gentleman named Rags.

The character list is dotted with many colorful sidekicks. For example, to list just a few, there's;

Stretch and Noaccount: two bums who have a part time job at the local funeral home. Together they stage a fake funeral while their boss is away on vacation.

Smitty: the huge bulk of a man with the heart of a boy who is the blacksmith at the village and who befriends Josh.

Tom and Belle: who take Joshua in as a youngster and care for him until he leaves for the Shaker village. Their warmth and compassion comes at perhaps the most critical time in Joshua's life.

The many brethren and sistren, as well as the elders at the Hancock village where Josh and Sara are raised are quite different and colorful as is their different way of life.

Mom: who is herself a surviving parent is institutionalized at a young age leaving Billy (Patches) without anyone except his newly found friend, Rags.

Barber John: provides a pivotal point and place for us to have the characters of our story meet and further provides us with an avenue to learn about the town and its gossip. He is a typical small town, old time barber. Billy works for him part time and Rags gets his hair cut there on a regular basis.

Squeaky the Mouse: a little mouse who adds character to our story.

The many Shaker children, the little girl friend of Sara, and the women who teach her to bake in the "good room" all bring a sense of goodness and innocence to our story. All in all the side characters provide us with the opportunity to expand our story in a more touching way and to relate it to family and community living in the "good old fashioned way".

Chapter 1
The Storm

A small horse drawn carriage carrying three people, a father, a mother, and a small boy, desperately tries to make its way through a blizzard on a snow covered, once open, country dirt road. Snow drifts are all around, and the blizzard increases as the cart tries to move forward and find the road.

Father: We can't go on. He won't go any further.

We hear the father speak as the snow builds high enough to stop the horse drawn cart. The drifts and wind begin to mount, pelting the boy, his father and his mother with continuous snow and sleet.

Father: (continues) It's no use…can't see! *(exclaims the father, trying to yell above the sound of the storm)* The wind… can't see through the wind. It's killing! Look over there…to the right. That light…may be a house…got to…got to get out and try to walk to it, we'll freeze to death out here!

We hear the words of the boy's father, desperately worried, exhausted and tired, as he tries to find some hope.

Father: Josh, get down first. And stay put! *(orders the father in an attempt to save his family)* Don't move till we all get down…damn, can't see a thing…you down boy? *(the father questions feverishly)*

Joshua: Yes papa. *(Joshua obediently replies)*

Father: O.k. Now stay put.

The father turns to help the mother, but she touches his hand and looks into his eyes. The father pauses, and looks deep into her eyes. He understands her look, then he turns again to the boy.

Father: Go to safety. *(says the father lovingly, pointing to the light far in the distance)*

The boy pauses unwilling to leave his parents.

Father: We'll follow. *(he says softly, the first time he has spoken this way to the boy)*

The boy hesitates at first, then obedient to his father's words, moves on as best he can toward the house in the distant darkness.

The father and mother watch in silence as their only son makes his way into the cold night, toward the light in the distance, the only safety they know.

With the boy now well on his way, the father gets down and tries to secure the wagon.

At that instant there is movement in the carriage.

The father pauses, standing up, realizing something is wrong.

The horse neighs, then pauses. We can see the snow begin to slide, slowly at first, then in one steady avalanche-like unfolding movement, engulfing everything with it, yet leaving the boy who now far in the distance stands and watches in disbelief and horror as the snow sweeps away the carriage and his parents into the ravine beyond the road.

The carriage and all the passengers are lost, leaving one young boy alone in an endless vastness of darkness, cold and snow.

Chapter 2
The Story Begins

In the midst of the dark and howling cold, the outline of a young boy can faintly be made out fighting to survive against the overwhelming odds of the bitter night. In the pitch black, the horror of the blistering winds can be heard as the blinding snow storm angrily shifts direction.

The pitiless darkness is broken only by a light coming from the window of a small desolate farmhouse. The light appears to the boy as a last glimmer of hope, a beacon in a harbor of terror in which he is now immersed and drowning. As if in a sea of snow the treacherous waves of wind and cold beat against the small child mercilessly. Fiercely and without warning entire snow drifts shift as the small boy, weak from the cold appears helpless against the terror of death which is so evident and patiently waiting in the wings of the darkness, waiting as if to claim the reward of its destruction. The boy is whirled from one direction to another as the sharpness of the biting cold cuts through, cruelly howling and raging like some mad dog made insane by the manic elements. The Northern wind swollen with terror combines its anger in an alliance with the bitter cold of the night against the boy's small frail body.

The same New England countryside which just a few months ago shown brilliant with sunshine and fields of flowers is now in the grip of the most horrendous blizzard in thirty years. Now the huge white drifts of snow with all of their ugly beauty weigh heavy upon the balance between life and death. The changing drifts and bitter forceful winds are too much for the lad and appear fatal to him in his attempt to navigate them. The boy struggles with all of his strength pushing ever forward toward the faint light which can be seen not far off. The house, which itself is nearly covered, illuminates the snow drifts, which partially cover, but which cannot exclude the light from the small windows. We can see the boy closer now. His frosted face is so reddened with wind burn that it's hard to distinguish it from the frozen blood upon his skin. The unbelievable force of the bitter wind fights and bites him, half turning his slender body as if he were an opponent in a boxing ring having received a devastating blow. Crippled by the cold in the night, he comes to what appears to be a fence. It can only be distinguished by the configuration of the snow as it swirls around it, giving us an occasional glimpse of the wooden rails beneath. In a final effort the small boy reaches out, grasping at it, only to fall short, disappearing beneath the swollen drifts of this black on white hell. Then miraculously, much as a fighter picking himself up off the canvas, he musters enough strength to pull himself up using the fence post to aid him. Against the blackness of the cold night air we can see through his heavy breath and frozen hair how very young he really is. A small ten, he is just a child, a David against the elements. He musters enough strength to pull himself up. As he does so, we can feel ourselves pulling with him. We see the streaks of blood left frozen by his fingers upon the fence post. The young boy fights forward, openly fearful and sobbing. He is alone and outnumbered and he knows it.

    Now it has become only a matter of which he will reach first, the door of the house with the light spilling out, or the door of death. The snow caught by the night's wind is lighted as it flies frantically about. He struggles for all that he is worth to reach a small hollow, made by the wind, just forward of the door. There he finds a respite from the vengeance of the night. As if in the hollow of God's own hand he rests for a moment trying to catch his breath. There on his hands and knees he remains for the moment amongst his own sobs and the terrible fear of this unyielding, relentless, terrifying time. Then with whatever strength he has left in his near frozen little body he again attempts to raise himself. With what appears to be his last given breath he barely calls out the word "…Help.…" But there at the door, and now totally exhausted, his tiny figure falls. His head and body crash against the door, as his last efforts surrender to the cold. Unable to continue, he slides down the door and lays there felled by the cruel wind. Beaten down by the angry cold he lay in a heap, in the black night, at the entrance.

Chapter 3
Inside the House

The inside of the house is small and warm, neat and cozy. It is a small country house, neatly kept and looking and feeling twice as warm as it would normally, because its warmth is in such contrast to the weather outside. There is a fire in the small fireplace. A black woman is walking across the living room with a quilt in her arms. As we look across the living room, and into the kitchen, we can see an older black man who is in his socks. He is lighting his pipe as he watches the coffee pot on the cast metal stove as it heats. Suddenly, as the woman passes near the front door on her way to a set of stairs that leads upstairs to the bedroom we hear a thud....she stops…looks toward the front door…then turns her head back again as if to continue on. Then we hear a scratching sound against the door as of a body falling. She turns again….this time she walks a step toward the door. Suddenly she senses that something is wrong much as a mother would sense her own child in trouble. She calls in a soft but slightly worrisome voice.

Woman: …..Tom…..(then a little louder and with more urgency as she hurries toward the closed door) …..Tom….. Tom!!!!!

Tom sensing her need in the urgency of her voice puts his pipe down and comes toward her. By now she has opened the door. As the door blows open the snow angrily intrudes into the warmth of the room bringing with it the fallen body of the youth. The howling bitterness of the wind is joined by the terror of the cry of the woman's voice against the night.

Woman: .....My God…..Tom…..Tom!!!!!

Tom out of instinct rather than by thought rushes down toward the frail and weather beaten body of the near frozen victim, snatches him up in his arms and in movements of complete urgency brings the small unconscious body to a couch near the fireplace. As Tom does this the woman is trying in vain to close the front door, but the wind and snow are too much for her. Tom rushes over to help her. As he does he starts to direct the woman, his wife, while at the same time he forces the door closed.

Tom: Belle…..water, Belle. Water….Get a basin of water…. Hurry!

She rushes into the kitchen. We hear the sound of clanging pans as she fumbles for a basin. We can hear and see her as she pumps water from the inside pump into the basin. Rushing out of the kitchen with a basin and a small wash cloth size rag in her hands she hurries over to the side of Tom who is with the boy. By now Tom has the boy nearly naked and wrapped in the quilt that the woman was carrying.

Tom: Get some water on him Belle…..Wash him down.

Belle: Tom…Tom, he's nearly blue.

Tom: I know, I know. Get him wet Belle, 'specially his fingers… his nose…ears. Got to get these shoes off… *(Tom hurriedly gets the boys shoes off and his socks also)*…got to get to those toes… those toes…he's frozen. Ah, Belle this poor creature is near froze. He's 'bout cold as death.

Tom reaches into the basin with his bare hands and wets down the boy's feet. He repeats this several times. As he does this Belle works at wetting down the lads near frozen body with the cloth. Her face is creased with worry. She rushes back to the kitchen to retrieve a towel and then back out again. She is worried, muttering to herself as she moves about. She goes about drying the boy's face and hair which is now fully wet from melted ice and snow.

Belle: Merciful God in Heaven…please…please help this helpless child. Oh God in Heaven…please…please God, please.

Both Tom and Belle continue to minister after the boy. Belle goes to the fireplace and holds some towels up against the warmth of the fire and wraps the boy's arms and legs to warm them. Tom rubs his hands together to warm them with the friction of the rubbing and then places his warm hands over the ears and hands of the boy. After warming the small lad Belle wraps him in the quilt. Then she takes the child now wrapped in the quilt into her arms and begins to rock him as if to give of her own warmth and love to his life.

It is later into the evening. Belle intent and tired has laid the boy on the couch near the fire. The night grows on in an almost endless calm. Both Tom and Belle remain awake and attentive over the little white baby like boy who is wrapped in the quilt. The light of the fire flickers as it reflects off of the still face of the youngster and shows upon the grim and worried tired black faces of both Belle and Tom.

Tom adds wood to the fire stoking and stirring it.

Tom: Got to get this fire hotter…Get this boy warm.

The night rolls on in stillness. We can see the concern of both Tom and Belle. The quietness and waiting is intensified by the quiet flickering of the fire throughout the night.

Tom realizing the tension and frustration of Belle moves over to her and quietly whispers to her.

Tom: (in a soft whisper) Is he breathing o.k.?

Belle: (in a soft voice looking down at, but speaking as if not to wake the child) Yes, Tom …Praise the Lord. But not even a twinge Tom. Not a movement of any kind.

Tom: Fever?

Belle looks down and with her upper arm she wipes her eyes as if wiping away a tear. Then she caresses his still brow with her hand.

Belle: Hard to tell. Poor child's face is so burned from the wind and cold.

As Belle says this the tears start to come down her cheeks. Tom reaches over and grabs her shoulder with his hand to comfort her.

Tom: Just keep believing woman…just keep believing. We've done as much as we can do for now.

The scene is later that night. Tom has fallen asleep still sitting up in a chair near the boy and the fire. In the fireplace lighted room Belle remains awake in the stillness of the long night. The night seems endless. Only the howling of the wind in the chimney of the fireplace remains a constant reminder of all that has gone on here tonight and of the treacherous conditions outside. The night passes slowly as Belle keeps her constant vigil over her newly found ward, looking patiently for any sign of improvement.

Morning is breaking now and the snow has stopped. The sun seems to be much brighter than it usually is as it reflects off of the snow in an almost blinding brilliance through the window, lighting up the start of a new day. The room is filled with a clean and innocent light which in its brightness seems to cancel out the horror of the night past. Tom is deep asleep in the chair, his head fallen to one side, and Belle who had dozed off for a short spell is awakened by the brightness of the welcomed morning light. She looks down at her ward. The boy is now laying on his side still wrapped in the comfort of the warm quilt. Suddenly the lines of worry and concern momentarily yield to a mixture of surprise and excitement. She starts to speak in a cracking half tired morning voice as she moves to where Tom is sleeping and gently shakes his arm.

Belle: …Tom…Tom…*(as she gently shakes his arm to wake him)*…Tom.

Tom arises still half asleep. Not yet fully awake, he is still attentive to Belle's action.

Belle: He moved…He's on his side Tom. He must have moved in his sleep. Thank God. He moved Tom.

Tom gets up from his chair. The smile on his face breaks the tense episode. It is catching, as Belle returns his smile. Tom grabs Belle and hugs her. They rock in each other's arms for a moment. Then Belle moves back to the lad. She softly sets herself on the floor beside the couch where she rests and softly brushes the hair from his face.

Belle: Beautiful child. Belle's gonna get you better. *(she looks up and smiles once again at Tom)*

Tom looks at Belle and shakes his head from side to side as if to say, "I don't believe this is happening". Then he goes to the kitchen where we saw him before this all started. Still in his socks he removes the cover from the coffee pot and peers in.

Tom: A little over cooked.

Looking over he picks up his pipe, puts it to his lips and lights it. Now blowing the smoke out as he holds the pipe in one hand he looks at it, then speaks.

Tom: Pipes still good.

He looks at it again. Then he places it back into his mouth and continues to puff.

Tom talks now in a questioning voice as he smokes his pipe.

Tom: Belle? What on earth do you suppose this child was doing out on a night like that?

Belle: I don't have the slightest idea, Tom. I can't even imagine. But I know one thing for sure…It can't be good.

Tom: How's he doing?

Belle: Better I think. He seems to have some color…Not as much as you and me, but at least he's got some.

With that they both enjoy a well-deserved laugh. They laugh in a quiet way so as not to disturb the child. Tom shakes his head in amazement.

Belle: You know something, Tom, he ain't been here but a few hours but it seems like forever. I feel like I know this beautiful child…Lord don't try me like this, I'm getting too old.

The boy remains asleep. He's a little dark haired fellow. And although beaten by the elements of the storm to within a fraction of death we can see what Belle means. The blessings of youth show through even the gravest misfortune.

It's later that same morning now and the two are busy doing what they can while still keeping an ever watchful eye on the youngster. Tom is dressed in his heavy coat and hat and has his hunting boots on.

Tom: I'm going to the hen house…if we still have one. Belle, you be alright?

Belle half nods and half smiles in acknowledgement as she

gets busier putting a few little things together just in case the lad wakes. There's some soup and some chicken heating just in case; some fresh cut bread and some milk warming just in case. She has a pot with some water heating. Now she reaches up to a shelf near her pantry and takes down a jar with some dry leaves in it. Opening the jar she takes some of the leaves and blends them into the pot of hot water. As she does this she bends and stretches as she leans to get her nose over the steaming pot. She sniffs it as if to test the smell.

Belle: Smells just right for someone his size. Chamomile herbs…good for your soul.

The brightness of the morning sun and the aroma of the preparation of food and tea have reached the sleeping boy. Soon there is a stirring in the quilt. The lad awakens, his eyes not yet opened.

There is a thrashing and a whimper which soon turn into a series of violent movements and a full mix of screaming and crying. His eyes not yet opened the boy is still living the nightmare of the night before, his body shivering with fright. Now in a screaming crying voice, panicked and frantic, the lad's eyes open but are not yet adjusted to the brightness of the light. He fights out of the quilt with its life giving warmth and calls out.

Boy: Mama….. *(crying and thrashing)*…..Mama…..Pa….. *(louder and louder)* …..Mama…..Papa…..Mama…..Pa…..

By this time the boy is in a panic. Belle rushes over to the lad. She grabs him up and holds him close in her arms. The boy only partially comforted, but fully confused, continues his panic sobbing. With this the front door opens. It's Tom. He looks very concerned. Knowing something that neither the boy nor Belle knows he comes to them. Then, his face strained from holding back the tears, he puts his arms around both of them pulling them closer together. Tom has just discovered why the boy was out on a night like last night alone in such a blizzard. He can no longer restrain his tears. He breaks from them and with his head down takes very large steps which put him in the kitchen. Once in the kitchen we hear Tom first break down in sobs and then this is followed by an awful retching sound as Tom strains bent over at the sink. After he has finished vomiting he pumps the handle to clear the sink; then he cups some water in his hand and washes out his mouth spitting it back into the sink. After this he wets his hands and rubs them over his face, then grabbing a towel he dries himself. As Belle continues to comfort the boy we see Tom open a cabinet door and take out a bottle. He then takes a glass from the sill of the window and retreats to the kitchen table. Pouring a drink he slumps back in his chair and swallows the drink. Then putting the empty glass on the table he grasps the edge of the table with both hands, his arms stretched out and stiff in front of him.

Tom sits at the table, just staring in front of him. Belle has comforted the totally exhausted boy back to sleep. She comes to Tom and stands in the doorway of the kitchen. She looks at him but he does not return her gaze. He just continues to look down at the table as if off from where he is – a great distance.

Belle: (softly and inquiring) ...Tom?

There is a pause. Without motion Tom sits in the safety of this momentary quietness. Then he speaks.

Tom: Their wagon...It went off the road...*(now looking up towards her)*...I guess they were knocked unconscious. The only thing left is the horse and he's suffering...*(now looking toward the boy)*...He couldn't help them...*(returning his gaze downward)*...must have been coming to try and get help...He's a brave little guy, Belle. *(pause and sigh)*

Tom rises from the table and reaches for his rifle above the back door. Taking it down he opens the chamber, reaches into his coat pocket and taking a bullet out loads it into the gun.

Tom: Got to take care of business, Belle. Can't let that animal suffer any longer. I've got to go to town and get some help…I'll be back before dark.

Tom puts his hat on and starts out the back door. Belle just turns in the doorway and holds onto the frame with both hands. She tilts her head against the wall and just looks motionless across the room in the direction of the young Joshua. She stares motionless in the silence. Without any movement or emotion of any sort she just waits in the silence. Then the silence is broken. The sound of the gun bluntly cuts through the air and into her heart. Still absolutely motionless and without ever changing her expression tears start to roll down her cheeks.

The scene fades.

Chapter 4
The Doctor's Visit

It is later that same day and we are a short distance from the small house of Tom and Belle. Two men on horseback are riding toward the house. The horses are up to their bellies in the deep, late day snow of the previous night. One of the riders brushes a branch away from his face as they pass beneath a snow laden tree. We recognize one of the riders as Tom. The other man is holding a small doctors bag in one hand. They ride up to the front fence where they dismount and rein the horses. Together they make their way to the house. Tom leads the way as the doctor follows. Once on the wooden steps in front of the house they stomp their feet and kick the side of the steps to remove some of the snow from their shoes. Tom opens the door and enters the house holding the door open for the doctor to follow. Once both men are inside they remove their coats and hats and hang them on wooden pegs near the entrance. Then they cautiously move across the living room to the kitchen where they find the boy and Belle. He is seated at the table. He is drinking some warm milk as Belle is placing some buttered bread on a plate in front of him. She looks up as the men enter the room.

Belle: Thank God. *(relieved)* You got back just in time. He wanted to go back out searching. Told him he needed something to keep up his strength first. Doctor.....Tom.….This is Joshua. *(they now know his name)*

Joshua continues to eat and drink. He is obviously starved.

Doctor: Good, he has an appetite. As soon as he finishes eating I'll get a look at him.

As Tom gestures both men move away from the kitchen toward the living room.

Tom: Doc, how about some coffee? Something stronger?

Doctor: Coffee'd be great Tom.

Tom moves back toward the kitchen.

Tom: Belle, think it'd be alright if I got…..

Belle hands Tom a tray with two cups of coffee on it and some fresh baked bread.

Belle: Here you go. *(as she hands it to him)*

Tom: (looking toward Belle) We got to have guests more often. Service is real good 'round here today.

Belle pays him no mind as he returns to the living room. The doctor is already seated in front of the fireplace enjoying its warmth. Then suddenly and without incident the young Joshua and Belle appear in the doorway to the living room. Joshua, who is small for his age is dressed in one of Tom's green and black checkered hunting shirts. The shirt hangs down below his knees. Belle puts her arm around the back of him as they approach the men. The doctor and Tom look up.

The doctor offers his hand to shake Joshes.

Doctor: (now shaking the outstretched hand of Josh) Joshua, I'm Doctor Williams. I'm very pleased to meet you. How are you feeling? Does anything hurt?

Joshua: (holding back his tears and fear) No sir…(pause)…. my face just a little. Where's Ma,…Pa?

The doctor does not answer for the moment but continues with the exam.

Doctor: That's a pretty nasty wind burn you've got there Josh...Well now, let's see what we can do about that... *(as he speaks the doctor looks and reaches into his bag)*...I've got some ointment in here...here it is...*(he retrieves a small jar with ointment in it)*...I want you to put this on your skin every day until it clears that redness...hmm...Got some cuts on your hands and face also...let's have a look...hmm...not too deep... Any pain?

Joshua: No sir,...just my face a little. *(he says again, quieter this time)*

Doctor: Josh, you seem to have some chills *(Josh shakes a little with chills)*...Let me check...hmm....*(he puts his hand on Joshua's brow)*

As the doctor checks Joshua's temperature, Belle wraps the quilt around him as the boy continues to shake intermittently.

Doctor: Josh I just want to check you over, make sure nothing is broken and that you're o.k. ...Sit over here.

Joshua sits on a chair as the doctor checks his toes and fingers, and his ears.

Doctor: That's the good blood of youth. No frost bite. Amazing...? *(he continues)*...Josh stand for a moment, please... 'Atta boy...*(as Josh hops down from the chair and stands)*.

With this the doctor pushes on the boy's inners checking out his liver, spleen, etc. As he pushes in one area Josh cringes a little.

Doctor: ...hmmm...

The doctor then gently pushes Joshua's head upward from under his chin to look into his mouth.

Doctor: Open…*(peers into his mouth)*…o.k., stick out your tongue…*(he depresses it with a stick)*…say, ahh…..hmmm……I'll tell you Josh…do you mind if I call you Josh?

Joshua: No sir.

Doctor: Well young man, you seemed a little sore when I pushed on your belly. It's probably just some bruises, but let's not take any chances. It's better to be sure. I've spoken to Tom about your staying here for a while until I'm sure you're alright. Will you do that for me?... I know they would love to have you stay. *(Belle looks down with a smile on her lips and nods yes).*

Joshua: Yes sir.

Doctor: Josh, you had a pretty bad time of it out there last night. I want you to stay indoors and I want you to get plenty of rest. Eat as much of Belle's good food as you can, but don't force your eating to start with. Belle, get a goodly amount of soup and fluids into this young man.

Joshua: Can I go out for just a little while? *(looking at Belle and pointing to his coat).*

Doctor: Why is that, Josh?

Joshua: To get Mama and Pa. I know if I were hurt they would come out and get me…I want to see them.

Doctor: (pause) I don't think that's such a good idea, Josh. I know what your mom would want right now.

Joshua: (slowly looking up) What would Ma want?

Doctor: She'd want you to get better, real fast… *(spoken gently)*…Mom is asleep Josh…I promise you Josh that Tom and I will take care of everything. There is no need to think about it. Try to forget. Everyone here loves you very much. You're safe, and nothing is going to happen to you. Everything is going to be fine. You just get better. That's what your mom would want and that's what we want.

Joshua: Yes sir.

Tom moves down to one knee to make himself shorter and looks straight into the eyes of Joshua.

Tom: (encouragingly) Look Josh...son... we're all here to help one another, and that's exactly what we're going to do. I promise you will not have to worry about anything except getting strong. We're all God's children, and we're all here to help one another. Belle and I already love you.

Doctor: I'll be by to see you again. We'll talk more. You go and rest now.

Belle: (as she gives Joshua a big hug) Come on young man...upstairs into the big bed.

They turn and start toward the stairs. Then Josh stops and turns to the doctor.

Joshua: Thank you, doctor.

Doctor: I'll be back soon, Josh.

The doctor waits as Josh and Belle ascend the stairs, then he turns to Tom while reaching and looking into his bag.

Doctor: Tom, I'm going to give you some powders that I picked up down at the Shaker village. If the boy can't sleep mix half a spoonful of powder with some warm milk and have him drink it. It will ease the memory of what went on. We just have to buy him some time. Time's the great healer in a case like this. There's a lot of hurt to be healed...God love'em. Take this bottle of cough medicine also just in case he starts to develop a cold. Those Shakers make a cough remedy that really works. They make the best pharmaceuticals in the entire country. We're lucky they're right nearby at Hancock. Have you ever seen their herb gardens down there, Tom? They grow most everything they use to make the remedies right there at the village...Amazing people. *(after a short pause)* Well, I best be getting back now. I'll send Timothy out to give you a hand with the other…*(referring to the accident)* and make arrangements.

Tom: What about later, Doc? What happens then?

Doctor: Later…? *(pause)*… Well I'll tell you Tom, the only place that I know of that takes in orphans is right there in Hancock…the Shakers. I'm sure they'll take him in. It's the only place around that takes kids in. But I'll tell you what, he'll find a good home there and have a good bringing up. They really are a good people. They have a fine school and they are a healthy and peace loving, God fearing people…a little strange to my way of thinking…but then again they seem to be a bit ahead of the rest of us about most things. But that's later…Now we just have to get him better. Tom, it sure is good of you and Belle to take care of him like this. Listen, if he has any problems just come on ahead and fetch me. If not, I'll stop back in a few days just to see how he's doing.

Tom: Thanks, Doc. It's getting late, do you want me to ride back with you?

Doctor: No need, thank you Tom. Old Lemon knows the way back home by heart. She knows there's a pail of oats waiting back there for her. She's alright *(as he puts his coat on)*. In fact that old girl has been so dependable I might have to make her a senior partner soon, but then she'd probably want to carry the bag and want me to carry her to my patients…and I hate oats.

Both men have eased their way toward the door which is open now, and the doctor is about to leave. Belle is seen coming down the stairs. She comes to the door also.

Belle: He's asleep, resting now.

Doctor: Good.

Tom acknowledges this also with a single nod, "yes".

Belle: Goodbye Doctor Williams, and thank you.

Tom: Thanks, Doc.

Doctor: 'Bye Belle…Tom. Say goodbye to Josh for me.

As the doctor leaves we can see his horse tied to the fence. She is a little more lemon colored than a palomino.

The scene ends as the door closes.

Chapter 5
Ain't Scared

Doc's office is in town. We are in the very small waiting room. There is an older couple sitting on the straight backed chairs fussing at each other.

Old Lady: You just scared.

Old Man: Ain't scared…Just careful.

Old Lady: (with a half laugh and half smirk on her face she waves her hand toward him) Scared….can't get no more scared than you are.

Old Man: Am not…you best mind your mouth old woman. All I know is that I'm alive out here with just a little bit of pain, and I know that better than being in there gittin' better with a whole lot of pain. Or maybe he's gonna get me so good with some secret treatment he ain't tried yet that they'll carry me out with no pain at all…BUT I AIN'T SCARED…just wish it were you instead of me. What's a wife for anyhow?

Old Lady: Maybe it's better if you wait then, 'cause when I get you home you gonna need him again.

With this the doctor's office door opens and a boy walks out with a dog in his arms. The dog has a leg that has been all bandaged up. The old man and the old lady look at each other. As they do the front door opens and Tom, Belle, and Josh walk in.

Doctor: Hi, Josh. How are you doing?

Old Man: Doc, you take the boy first. I ain't in no hurry.

Doctor: O.k. Come right on in Josh.

Josh walks into the doctor's office and the door closes. With this the old man and old lady get up and urge Tom and Belle to be seated in the only two chairs. As they do, they make their way to the door and open it. They pass through the doorway and just prior to closing the door the old man sticks his head back in.

Old Man: Just tell him that we were in a hurry.

The door is now closed but we can still hear them talking through it.

Old Lady: Even the dog has more courage than you. *(voices fade out)*

Belle and Tom just look at each other. Tom shakes his head....

Belle: Oh, Lord.

A short period of time goes by as Belle and Tom wait in the outer room. There in the quiet, not a word is spoken. From time to time they look at each other in a quiet confident way sensing that at least the danger of physical harm is past. Confidently they wait knowing that everything will be alright. Then the door opens and the boy and doctor come out. Josh even has a slight smile on his face. He approaches Belle as if he has accomplished something. We can see that his color has returned to normal, that his repair is well underway.

Doctor: He is healing very fast....You're doing a good job, Josh. *(Joshua smiles)*

All then walk to the door as a group as they exit.

All three: 'Bye doctor...thank you.

Doctor: He's fine. Call me if you need me for anything.

Then the doctor comes back to his empty waiting room. He looks in the direction of where the old man and old lady were sitting. He pauses, seeing they are gone. He shakes his head…

Doctor: …..hmmm…..

Chapter 6
Yard Work

It is early morning and Tom and Josh are already out in the backyard mending the fence around the hen house. Most but not all of the snow is melted. We can see as Josh helps Tom, even with the eagerness of a ten year old boy, that he has fully recovered and has regained the brightness of his youth. As he hands Tom some wire and tools we hear Belle call to them from the house.

Belle: Tom, Josh...come on in now... have some breakfast.

Tom: Just a minute Belle. *(as he puts the finishing touches to a repair)* There, that ought to hold'er. What do you think partner?

Joshua: ….Yep…

There is a short pause.

Tom: Hey, Josh.

As Tom speaks he picks up a large green object from the garden, and walks back a few yards away from Joshua into a large field, while gesturing to a large stick near Joshes feet. Joshua picks up the stick with enthusiasm. It's obvious they have done this before.

'Smack' as bits and pieces of cabbage go flying. Josh is what would be the equivalent to being "at bat". There in the middle of last year's cabbage field Tom is pitching in old heads of cabbage underhand to Josh. Josh armed with a bat like stick is demolishing the cabbage heads as Tom deals them up.

Tom: Got that one past you.

Joshua: Lucky…it wasn't ripe enough.

'Smack' as Joshua hits another.

Tom: Last one!

Joshua: I'm going to hit it out of the field!

'Smack', another cabbage bites the dust…

Joshua and Tom walk in off of the cabbage field.

Tom: You know, Josh, it wouldn't surprise me if one day they make up a game like that.

Joshua: A game? What sort of game?

Tom: You know, like a sport.

Joshua: A sport? *(pause)* What would they call it?

Tom: I don't know…*(pause)*….cabbage ball….?

Joshua: (pause) …oh….

They both laugh.

Tom: Let's get some breakfast.

Both then pick up their tools and walk toward the house. As they approach the back door Tom stamps his feet to clean off some of the earth that clings to his shoes. In a copycat manner then Josh repeats the same exact movements with his own shoes. Both then sit down on the back wooden steps and take off their shoes. Shoes in hand they enter the house and move into the kitchen.

Belle: Wait 'till you see what Belle's done cooked this morning….ummm, ah!

Tom: Ooh woman, that sure is just the right aroma to greet a hungry man's nose.

Belle: Tom, one of these days I'm going to put you on a diet.

Tom: As long as it ain't today. *(as he snatches a piece of muffin from the table)*

Belle: (turning in the direction of Josh) Don't forget, wash up real good before you eat…*(Josh has already spilt something on his shirt, Belle turns and sees it, then adjusts her statement)*… and after you finish.

Tom: Don't want to wash up too good. Boys got to eat a little dirt if he wants to grow.

Belle: Tom! You stop talking that nonsense. If that were true, you'd be a giant.

Tom: Josh, old Tom just kiddin'. But truth is, unclean thing don't come from outside a man that can hurt him. Only thing that can hurt you is if the dirt comes from the inside. Tom's talking truth now Josh.

Belle: Josh, while you and the Apostle Tom eat your breakfast I'm going to go upstairs and put out your clean clothes. Now don't forget…before and after.

Then Belle makes her way upstairs. We follow her as she enters the main and only bedroom. Going from the closet to the dresser she systematically puts out their clothes. Then she puts a traveling case on the bed and starts to fill it with all of Joshes belongings, which don't amount to a whole lot. She holds up the small trousers and each item to follow as she neatly folds and packs them away into the traveling case. Holding the last item, a small pair of blue jean coveralls, she sits on the edge of the bed. Still sitting she now holds them in her arms close to her body. There she sits for the moment. Then with a large sigh she stands and packs them into the case also.

Tom has come upstairs. He is standing in the doorway.

Belle is folding a small shirt.

Tom: He's downstairs finishing up now.

Belle: (still holding the shirt) Guess I kinda wished this day would never come…*(pause almost in tears)*… but…here it is.

Belle continues folding the shirt and places it on the case.

Belle: Tomorrow my Joshua leaves….Oh Lord give me strength…*(pauses then continues)*…Where does the time go?

Tom: (says caringly) He's been with us almost the entire winter.

Belle: (pauses again) In a way I'm so proud we were blessed with him. I guess we were here when we were needed. *(she is almost in tears)*

Tom: It's hard to give up what you love.

Belle: That's the way of life though isn't it Tom?

Tom: Yes Belle, that's the way life goes. Let's be thankful for what we have while we have it.

Belle: One step taken, one step gone.

Tom: And every season in its place. Funny a little guy like that can make such a difference. It's better though Belle. He'll get the proper education, and we will see him.

Belle: As often as we see him now?

Tom: (pause) I wish. He's my working buddy you know.

Belle: I noticed.

Tom: (moves to Belle and embraces her) I love you Belle. You're my woman.

Belle: My Tom. I love you…and so does Joshua.

After a moment they separate from their embrace.

Tom: I better get downstairs.

Belle just nods, "yes". Tom understands as he just leaves Belle to her privacy of that moment.

Tom descends the stairs and walks toward the kitchen. Pausing for a moment Tom takes a deep breath before entering the room as if to prepare himself to meet Joshua in a relaxed manner. Joshua is seated at the breakfast table and by now has almost finished eating. Even though they have finished, the table still looks so good as to be almost joyful, with its bounty of fresh biscuits, bacon, sausages, grits and eggs against the background of dishes, cups, and glasses. Tom's chair is still a little back from the table, as he seats himself by sliding and jockeying into place. We hear the sound of Joshua's fork and knife as he lets them lightly fall into his almost entirely empty dish.

Joshua: I'm stuffed.

Tom: It's important to eat a good breakfast. You got a lot of growing to do yet. Got to feed the fire. *(laughing)* From the looks of that dish you about ready for another day's growing.

Joshua: If I grow as much as I've eaten, I'm going to be a giant like you.

Tom: You're already a giant. *(pause)* You know what today is?

Joshua: Yep…It's church going day.

Tom: Yep…and then tomorrow we go down to the Shaker village and meet your new friends. But first, we go to church… today.

Joshua: Tom?

Tom: Yes, Josh.

Joshua: Do you think that it would be alright if after church we go to visit Mama and Papa on our way to the village.

Tom: Of course. Belle and I are sure going to miss having you around here you know.

Joshua: I'm going to miss you and Belle…*(pause)*…Tom?… *(another question)*

Tom: Josh?

Joshua: Do I have to go?

Tom: The way this crazy world is right now Josh, it's probably better. Besides we ain't going nowhere. Belle and I, *(putting his big hand over Joshes hand)*, we'll be seeing you all the time.

Chapter 7
In Our Prayers

The scene ends and the next scene opens with the three of them on Tom's open wagon pulling out of the yard. We watch them as they pass along the wet, early spring road. We watch the wagon as it moves into the distance. We see the same wagon approaching us up a small hill. Just as it climbs over the hill it pulls to the side and stops. Josh is very fast to jump out and runs ahead. Both Tom and Belle also get down from the wagon. As they do we can see Josh running ahead. It is early spring and evidence of both winter and spring are present as the grass about the area is green while the ground is still wet and spotted with the remains of small, still lingering, occasional piles of wet white snow. The once awesome drifts have now been reduced to an occasional coarse pile here and there, and are now subject to the will of the new and increasing spring sunshine. Josh comes to a headstone and stops. The earth is mounded in front of it. There the mix of earth and new grass combine. The grave is recent. There is a small wooden cross near the head of it. Josh, standing like a little soldier in front of the mound and headstone speaks as if his parents could hear him. His voice is steady and calm. His voice is not sad but has an almost joyful sound to it as if he were really talking directly to them. He is for the lack of a better description loyally loving and happy that he is with them. It is as if he could feel the presence of their love. This is what shows in his voice as he speaks.

Joshua: Mama…Papa…*(pause)*…I have come to see you today and to tell you about the good things that are happening. *(he says this in a way as to almost try to cheer them up and reassure them that everything is o.k.).* I really do miss you Mom and Pa…really I do. *(pause)* Belle says that one day we will all be together and happy again. *(shorter pause, then his voice is a little more hurried and slightly more excited).* She said that right now you're just asleep and that when you wake up that you will find yourself being held in the arms of Jesus. I talk to him every day Mom, and I ask him to hold on real tight to both you and Dad so that you don't fall. *(pause with a thoughtful look on his face).* Ma…he must have pretty big arms to hold all of us and not to drop anyone. He must really be strong. I've decided that I want to be just like him. Then I could hold you too. *(longer pause)*…Ma,…Pa…*(his voice saddens)*…today I'm going to the Shaker village to live… *(he looks down and his voice softens).* I don't know when I'll be able to come back again to see you *(sighs).* Today I helped Tom mend the chickens' fence, and I'm all better, just like the doctor said you'd want me to be *(pause).* Doc and everyone says that the Shaker village is a great place to live. There are lots of kids there and I'll have a lot of friends. Ma,…Pa…I think of you all the time. Jesus, please hold Ma and Pa for me so we can be together.

We see that both Tom and Belle have been quietly standing behind Josh at the grave site. Tom reaches out with his right hand and places it gently on the left shoulder of Josh.

Tom: I think we'd better go now Josh, the Elder Harris will be waiting. He's expecting you early afternoon.

With this Josh pauses for a moment and then gently gets down on his knees. He folds and presses his hands together bowing his head. He prays to himself for a moment, then stretching both arms forward and opening his hands, he places them on the grave site in front of him. Both arms are spread, one hand over his mother and the other over his father. He speaks.

Joshua: Mama…Papa…I love you …Goodbye.

Then Joshua rises. Without turning he reaches up for the hands of Belle and Tom. They all stand together there in silence for a moment longer. Then Josh lets go of their hands. Tom has been holding Joshua's hat in his left hand. Josh takes the hat and puts it on. Belle and Josh then walk off toward the wagon and Tom lingers behind. Tom has his own hat now in his hand. He takes just a few short steps forward and stops.

Tom: (looking down at the grave) I never had the pleasure of meeting you. Your boy Joshua…he's a beautiful child. You know if things were different, Belle and I would be proud to raise him up. Short time he's been with us we've grown to love him. The people he's going to be with…they a good people. Belle and I, we be sure to keep him in our hearts…Promise.

Tom then replaces his hat onto his head, then fixing himself and brushing his jacket he begins to walk back toward the wagon. Josh and Belle are already seated up on the wagon waiting for him. Tom walks around to his side of the wagon. Looking up at Josh and smiling he speaks to Josh.

Tom: All aboard.

Then he jumps up into the wagon and taking the reins into his hands prepares to gently snap them on the horse's rump. But he stops. He looks over to Joshua.

Tom: How'd you like to drive?

Joshua: Me?

Tom: Well there are only two men on this wagon, so I guess I mean you.

Joshua: Wow!

Tom: Come on, sit over here. I'll show you how. 'Atta boy! Take the reins like this…that's right. Now wrap your finger… like this. That's good. Now gently let the horse feel the reins very lightly and give 'em the go ahead with your voice at the same time…Get up! There you go, nothing to it.

With that the wagon slowly drives away.

Chapter 8
The Shaker Village

As the wagon slowly moves off we see the ever increasing view of the countryside with its trees and last fall's leaves, brown and lifeless, fallen like some old garment about the roots, which have now just begun to bring forth new life from the same earth that also holds both parents of Joshua.

Similarly we have the effect of a boy leaving one world to become a man in another, ever growing, ever increasing in size and scope.

From a distance we can see the wagon slowly and steadily advancing up the gradual grade of a distant hill. The wheels of the wagon turn so fast, they appear just a blur on the road. The wagon reaches the top of the hill and peers over the other side from the top.

The scene as we descend is Massachusetts. We are on a road in the beautiful Berkshires, full of color. It is spring and every field and every hillside is ablaze with the glory of the season. The briskness in the weather is quieted by the beauty and warmth of the golden sun upon every field, and barn, and grazing cow.

We are at the Shaker Village. The setting is the neat, clean community, with its small communal buildings of white, and tan, and red. The all wood and all brick buildings although different in their composition and structure are all so very much the same in their neatness and orderly appearance. Whatever their makeup it is evident that they are all of the same community. The bland red brick residence halls, wood working shops, and stone barn are surrounded by beautiful manicured farm pasture, orchards and spice gardens. Being it is Sunday there is no one at work but the evidence that work has been done is obvious in the fact that in spite of a long hard winter the community is already so much in order that it would appear that perhaps the winter by-passed this village.

The focus picks up two little girls as they run toward a tree swing which hangs by two ropes from the sturdy branch of an old apple tree, which is now fully in bloom. One girl is ahead of the other and as she scampers to the tree she jumps up onto the swing seat. The other, catching up, starts to push the swing. The second little girl pushes the swing several times and then gives the swing one very hard push. Laughing and giggling as she pushes the swing she calls out in a laughing, accusing manner.

Little Girl: Sara has a boyfriend. *(in an almost singing voice)*

Sara now starts dragging her feet to stop the swing. The other little girl still laughing and giggling turns and runs. Sara finally stops the swing and for a brief moment spurts out in pursuit of her little friend. However, she realizes that the other girl has gotten too much of a head start and so after a brief burst of chase she stops in frustration as the other little friend runs off.

Sara now looking in the direction of her friend yells out to her.

Sara: I do not! *(then talking to herself as if to defend herself)* When I grow up I am going to be an eldress. I'm going to cook in the "good room" and I'm going to sew and weave and…uugh…wash clothes and…and make remedies from herbs and…and go to the "good room" …*(now skipping and running off in the direction of the "good room")*…to get some cookies.

Sara continues to skip and run off to the "good room", which is located at the bottom of the residence building. It is here that all of the communal cooking is done. Arriving at the building she pulls the door open using both hands. As she enters the women are busy baking and cooking for the evening meal. Sara goes over to where a woman is making and baking. There are many freshly baked cookies on the table where the woman works. They are fresh from the hot brick ovens.

Sara: Sister Emma, may I ? *(as she looks toward the cookies)*

Sister Emma: With God's blessing child. Remember though, love comes from giving and not from getting. And then you be off. Off now to your chores. To the upstairs wash room with you. There are clothes that need hanging out.

With this Sara exits out of the residence building through the side door with her cookie in hand and playfully skips and works her way over to the laundry building. The washing, or laundry building, is much like the residence building in outward appearance in that they are both brick. The residence hall is however a three story building and the laundry building is a shorter two story structure. The washing area is located in the western half of the building and the pipe making and machine works are located in the eastern half of the same building. Sara enters downstairs where the laundry is being washed. There on the main level are super large kettles of water which are continually being heated over a very large open fireplace. Not far from the fireplace is a long machine which actually is four or five washing tubs with agitators all attached one to another so that all of the machine's action is automatic in that when one works they all work together. It is the first automatic washing machine. Nearby are several smaller kettles that will be used to transfer the hot water from the larger kettle to the tubs of the machine. Sara pauses as they transfer the water into the tubs and watches as the wheel-pulley device which is common to all the agitators is put into action. There is a large mound of wet wash which has previously been laundered near a dumbwaiter on one end of the room. The dumbwaiter is lowered and two women are busy now putting the new wash onto it. Sara runs over to the area and tries to hitch a ride up to the second floor, but a woman who has been loading the elevator turns and half scolds her for her attempt.

Washer Woman: The stairs young lady!

Sara skips to the stairs and ascends to the second floor where the dumbwaiter is just arriving. Up there on the second floor of the building several young girls and boys are leisurely hanging up wash over lines that have been strung across the large open space of the second floor. Sara walks over and starts to remove the wet wash from the elevator. With her arms full of laundry she starts to walk toward the area where they are hanging the wash up. Arriving at the area where the clothes are hanging she places the new wash on a flat wooden table top. As she returns to pick up more wash she passes the large window. Looking out she sees a wagon pulling into the front courtyard off of the main road. There is a driver and a young boy on the front seat. The one horse wagon is simple, and plain, and neat as is everything else there in the small village. The other children come over to see whatever it is that Sara is watching.

Child #1: That's the new boy.

Sara: What new boy?

Child #2: The new orphan boy from the city. Hear tell he lost both parents in an accident.

Sara: Oh. *(quiet sorrow in her voice)*

As the wagon passes through the front yard it passes beyond the end of the building and out of sight of the front window. But just as it went out of sight of the front window it comes into view through the rear window. We follow the wagon as it pulls up to the blacksmith and livery area. A rather large man eases out of the shop and takes the reins of the horse. He is cheerful and wearing a large leather apron over his coveralls and rolled up shirt sleeves. The driver gets down and walks around to the other side of the wagon. He reaches into the back of the wagon and removes a satchel containing some of the boy's belongings. Then in a calm and peaceful voice he speaks to the boy.

Driver: Come on Josh…this is it. Welcome home. *(as he helps the boy down).* What God sees fit to share with us, we're privileged to be able to share with you.

The driver then turns to the rather large man.

Driver: Smitty…..this here is Joshua.

Smitty, a horse of a man, walks over to the boy, bends at the waist and shakes his hand. Then he lifts the boy up abruptly and puts him on his shoulders. He then looks up into the boy's face and says with a smile and with pride;

Smitty: Come on, I'll show you my "smith shop" and some of the finest horses in all the East. Do you ride…? No matter. If you don't, you will. I'll teach you myself, not only to ride but to shoe a horse as well.

The driver has led the horse and wagon off and is now out of the picture. Smitty walks over to the open door of his shop with the boy still on his shoulders. At the entrance to the barn he lets Josh down off his shoulders and calls out to someone inside.

Smitty: Eddie.

A young boy much like Joshua walks out. He is slightly soiled from working but is obviously quite happy and at ease.

Smitty: Eddie, this is Joshua…your new brother.

Eddie: Hi, Joshua, I'm Eddie…..Welcome home.

Smitty: Eddie, why don't you take the rest of today off. Go get yourself cleaned up; help Joshua with his things and show him around. Help him get settled. Take him over to the elder brother Harris and find out what arrangements have been made for his room.

Eddie picks up Joshua's bag and they start toward the meeting hall.

Eddie: We're going over there Josh. *(pointing with the bag toward a white wooden building across the road.)* That's the meeting and fellowship hall where we worship. Elder Harris has his quarters above the hall.

Smitty: (Smitty yells after them) And after that take him down to the "good room"…Got to get some meat on them bones, lest he waste away to nothing like me…Ha,ha,ha,ha….

We see the boys walking toward the building as we see Smitty holding his sides enjoying his own joke. As they approach the building, there are two entrances; one to the left and one to the right, at opposite ends of the front of the meeting hall. They approach the entrance to the right and stop.

Eddie: This is the brethrens entrance. It's the entrance we use. The sisters use the other entrance.

Eddie now reaching down takes off his shoes. As he does so he speaks.

Eddie: Come on.

As he says "come on" his shoes are off. Joshua starts to remove his shoes, too.

Rags

Eddie: No need…yours are clean. Mine, well, between the horses and the ashes….not so clean.

As they ascend the stone steps of the small white wooden building and enter into the foyer they are met by stillness, quiet and sunlight which seems to fill every corner leaving nothing to the shadows. Even the floor and the staircase which faces them shines in the clean still light which fills the building. As Josh gazes to his left, his glance takes him through an open doorway into a rather large peaceful looking room. The room is painted blue and white, the colors most used by the Shakers. The trim is a sky blue and the walls of plaster are as smooth as a mirror and as white as the clouds. Josh can see that every window in the room is so clear that it appears as though there is no glass in the window panes. The room is flawless in simplicity and cleanliness. Every item in the room is in order. In the center of the room is a pair of candle wheels which are held to the ceiling by a rope. The rope extends down to the side wall at an angle and is tied there to a fastener. From this position the candle lights can be raised or lowered at will. Benches outline the perimeter of the room which is evenly divided into equal halves. Across the openness of the room, Josh can see the sisters entrance at the opposite end of the meeting room.

Joshua: Eddie, what's this room?

Eddie: It's our meeting room Josh. Do you mind if I call you Josh? *(Josh nods)* This is where we believers have our Sabbath worship. Each week we all come together here, the brethren on one side of the room, and the sistren on the other. We dance and sing and praise God in manifestation and have our service. We all share and give thanks together.

Joshua: What is manifest?

Eddie: It's easy; it's great; you'll see. God gives you a great gift of Himself; His spirit. Then you can manifest that same spirit he has given each of us, by speaking in tongues, healing, prophesy, word of wisdom and so on. That's how we receive the fruit of the spirit and why everyone here is so full of love and peace. You'll learn all about it. It's great! Come on, we'd better go now.

The boys ascend the immaculate stairs to the upper level of the meeting house. It is here that the elders live. The upper floor is separated into separate rooms, which are separated by the center hallway containing the staircase. Each of the rooms is furnished with typical Shaker furniture. The lines are clean and straight. There is no excess in Shaker life. A bed, a dresser, a chair and a simple table are all the essentials needed for their simple way of life, a life of efficiency and simplicity. Simplicity and perfection come together here in perfect union. As they walk through the floor and stand there at the head of the stairs in the hallway, Eddie walks over and knocks on the already open door of Elder Harris.

Elder Harris: (looking up from what he is writing) Good day to you, Eddie. God bless.

Eddie: (cheerful) Good day to you Elder Harris, and God bless.

Elder Harris: And this must be Joshua.

Eddie: Yes.

Elder Harris: Welcome home and God love and bless you Joshua.

Joshua: (shy, his voice cracking) Thank you, sir.

Elder Harris: I know you've had a long ride. You must be a little tired. Eddie, I've arranged for Joshua to stay at the main residence hall on the third floor. Josh, you go with Eddie. He'll show you the way and help you get settled in. After you've washed up a bit, had some supper and a good night's rest you will feel like a different person. Come by tomorrow after breakfast and we'll talk some more.

Eddie: Thank you, Elder Harris.

Joshua: Thank you, sir.

Elder Harris: Eddie…..Josh…..

The boys walk out of the room and they bound down the stairs bursting out of the meeting hall building. As they burst through the brethrens door Eddie stoops to pick up his shoes and while still half running and half hopping he fumbles to put his shoes on while still in motion. While doing all of this he is talking to Joshua at the same time.

Eddie: We're going to cross the road and go over to that big red brick building across the way.

With that they pass through the gate opening of the neat white fence and head toward the four story red brick residence building just on the other side of the road. As young boys would they hasten across the front lawn of the residence area and enter the building which like the meeting hall is absolutely spotless. Eddie turns to Joshua as they enter and appeals to his competitive spirit.

Eddie: Come on. I'll race you to the third floor.

As Eddie says this he puts his arm around Josh, across and grabbing Joshua's shoulder. Eddie is a little taller than Josh and does this in a gesture to make Joshua feel welcome.

Both boys bound up the stairs, laughing and intent on a bit of boyish competition as they climb faster and faster upward, flight by flight. But just as they are about to round the corner of the second floor, Joshua slams right into Sara who is on her way downstairs. Both end up on their fannies on the second floor landing. Sara, who was on her way downstairs, sits on the floor in shock. Eddie laughs out, loudly, pointing at them as they sit, done in by each other.

Sara: 'Taint funny, Eddie.

Sara picks herself up and Joshua does the same.

Joshua: I'm sorry, I …I didn't mean to…

Sara: (Sara interrupts) It's o.k....*(pause)*…I'm Sara… I live here in the family residence on the second floor.

Eddie: Sara, this here is Joshua. He's gonna live up on the third floor with the good guys.

Sara: We women are every bit as good as you men. Elder Aggie says so…*(pause)*…I'm pleased to meet you, Joshua…I'm Sara…*(she starts down the stairs)*...Welcome home…*(she takes another two steps and looks back)*...and God bless.

Joshua: (in a natural, but shy voice) Nice to meet you also, Sara. *(now in a self-conscious and shy voice)* …Bless you, too.

Chapter 9
Planting Corn

There is a residence hall with a long hallway. We can sense that it is truly a part of the Shaker way as the hallway glows in the brightness of the sunlight that bounds in through the windows at opposite ends of the hall. The entire building has been planned so as to take advantage of the natural light, and its design has been justified as the beauty of the natural light from without abounds within the entire residence building. As we move down the hallway we approach the open doorway of a room. As we peer in we can see that the dual windows, one on each wall, let in the brighter light which now illuminates the simplicity and neatness of the room's content. Between the bed and the window, against the wall stands a very small table of wood which itself sits on the wooden floor. Atop the table is a bowl and pitcher for washing. Above the table hanging from a single wooden peg is a towel. There is a small rope rug in front of the small single bed. The figure of a lad turns slowly in bed toward the light. It is Joshua now a little older. He rubs his eyes as he begins to awaken. Slowly at first he seems to come into the reality of morning, rubbing and stretching into the start of the new day. Then, suddenly with all of the realization of where he is and what time it is he pops up into a sitting position in bed as if propelled by a spring device. He looks around astonished, realizing that he must be the only one left in the residence hall. This is reinforced by the stillness and quiet of the building.

He kicks his light blanket off and jolts out of bed. Bolting to the wash basin he quickly splashes water on his face and quickly dries it with the face towel hanging from the wooden peg without ever removing it from its place. Then with one motion he moves like a cat to a solitary wooden chair where his blue trousers hang waiting neatly folded over its spoked back. Hurriedly he puts his trousers on. Next to go on is the white shirt that he cannot get to go under his belt fast enough. As he stuffs the loose ends into the waist of his pants he uprights his work shoes which are on the floor next to the chair with his bare feet. Then managing to get his work shoes on and tied, and as he spurts toward the door, he reaches out and grabs his straw brimmed hat which has been waiting for him neatly hung on a peg next to the exit. Pushing the hat on his head he leaves the room. Then as suddenly as he left the room we see him return. Obviously he has forgotten something. Removing his hat he runs toward the bed where he falls to his knees at its side and hurriedly mutters the words of a hasty prayer.

Joshua: Thank you Lord for this day….Amen.

He bolts up quickly and adjusts his hat back on his head once more as he rushes from the room. He literally bounds down the staircase several steps, and groups of steps at a time. Never stopping, he is in a continuous descent as he flies down the stairs. At the bottom without a moment's hesitation he bounds out through the screen door as we hear it slam open and squeak shut. He jumps down the three steps at the entrance and starts running across the back lawn and yard of the building grounds holding his hat on his head as he goes. As he moves we get a glimpse of everything around him which is so typical of Shaker life, being incredibly and indescribably neat, perfect and in order. The grass, the fences, the road, and the trees that line it are like part of a neat and painted portrait.

The sun is now fully up and growing in intensity. In the

distance on a grassy hillside we can see the small figures of a dozen or more souls abiding in the shade of a very large shade tree. Some are standing and some are leaning on hoes, and shovels, and rakes. Others are in pairs just talking and sitting while still others lay on the grass in the cool of the morning shade. We can see a small figure running like crazy across the field toward the group. In the background we can just see the roof of the residence hall very far off. Panting, Joshua arrives at the group. Those present don't even seem to notice. Without even one word being spoken upon his arrival, they all seem to get up and start to gravitate toward one rather lean and bearded man who is standing near the trunk of the big shade tree. There they gather together. All are in the shade of the tree now. It is obvious that they have been waiting for Joshua to arrive, but none have mentioned it. Joshua is in the rear of the gathering. A man next to him reaches out and puts his arm around Josh's shoulders. They all have now come together about the man who is obviously their leader.

Worker: (quietly as he looks toward Joshua with a smile) Morning Josh.

To Joshua's amazement there is no mention of his tardiness. The love and peace of these people prevail. Now all gathered, the tall and lean bearded man speaks.

Bearded Man: Good morning and God bless. Would someone open this beautiful day with a prayer of thanksgiving.

Worker: Most Heavenly and Gracious Father, we here gathered thank you for this beautiful day and for all the abundance you share with us on each and every occasion. Even at times when we forget, you Father never forget. Guide our hands and our way that in each and everything we do, we glorify you Father. And that all we do is according to your good will and pleasure. Guide us in your sufficiency. We thank you

Father as we enter this day with joy and confidence in the name of your son, our Lord and Savior Jesus Christ. Amen.

Bearded Man: We are all of one body. If one member of the body hurts we all hurt. If one member of the body rejoices we all rejoice. And if one member be late; well then we all just use the time to relax and enjoy the beauty of God's day just a little bit longer. Even the smallest member is a joy to the body and equally as important to its function and well worth waiting for. …Now then…"Hands to work and Hearts to God."

The entire group is dressed in blue and white. This is traditional for the Shaker community. All are men and most are wearing the typical straw hat. Now carrying their hoes and rakes they leave the shade of the large tree and walk along the farm road. To the side of the road the fields abound with corn and sunflower plants, full grown. As they walk along we notice that the plants of the fields are getting shorter. The younger and newer fields are growing but are not as yet fully mature. Soon they are upon a new field that has not as yet been planted. We can see in the center of the field a group of three men standing. They are talking and waiting. Our group is in no rush as it approaches them. Now as they all come together there is a polite shaking of hands and greetings. The bearded man addresses the three.

Bearded Man: Is that it? *(gesturing toward a small machine which is mounted on two large iron wheels)*

Ben: This is it! Put the finishing touches to 'er last night and we're ready to go.

Bearded Man: If you're ready, we're ready. What should we do?

Ben: Well, this is how it works *(pointing to a funnel like container on top of the machine)*. Keep this container filled with seed corn. You'll need another two people, to push her with these two handles. See then, as the wheels turn, it turns the drum and lets the seeds fall through these little openings here, while the spikes out front over here punch holes in the earth. Now then, as the wheels turn, the cylinder that feeds the corn turns, and the seed is dropped through this opening here and into the hole made by the spikes in the ground. We'll need several brethren to follow and cover over the seeds with earth using their hoes and rakes…And that's all there is to it.

Bearded Man: Excellent!... Excellent!

Another Worker #1: Should make planting a lot more pleasant.

Another Worker #2: You mean no more bending over in the hot sun to put those little yellow buggers into those silly little holes?...Praise God!

Bearded Man: Well brothers…Let's give it a try. If your invention works Ben, this will be a day to remember.

The bearded man grabs one handle as another worker grabs the other handle. Joshua runs up and takes a scoop of corn seed from an open sack on a nearby small wagon. Balancing the seed in the scoop he approaches the machine. Looking to the man at its side he receives acknowledgement to fill the bin atop the machine. He smiles as he fills the bin.

Everyone gathers closer as they begin to push the machine. The two iron wheels turn as the spikes dig into the earth. As the hole is made in the earth the machine moves forward and a seed drops into the hole. Everyone murmurs as the procedure repeats itself over and over. And as each seed drops the group begins to cheer. Everyone stops for the moment and they go over to Ben and pat him on the back, shake his hand, and congratulate him. Joshua throws his hat into the air. Ben is all smiles. He has done it. The first seed planting machine ever has just been invented and used. Soon the group is back to pushing and planting. Some follow covering the seeds with earth, while others feed in the seed, and while still others take turns pushing.

Soon they have finished planting, and the entire group moves back down the road that led them to the field originally. Joshua and another young lad are pushing the machine which now moves easily over the smooth dirt road. The men are talking as they go.

Bearded Man: Ben, it would have taken a full day, or longer, and a great deal more effort to have planted that field in the ordinary way.

Ben: Yep…But now we can plant it in the Shaker way.

Both men laugh with pride.

Soon they are approaching the same place that they started out from. The big tree, still there in the heat of the day, is offering its shade to the grass below. But now there are three young girls beneath the tree. At the side of the road is a small light cart. Beneath the tree is a small table with a pitcher and glasses on it. Soon they have all arrived back to enjoy the shade of the tree. The men all take glasses as the three young girls fill them up. Straw hats tilted back the men drink and are refreshed from the heat and thirst of the day. Joshua, copying the older men, tilts his hat back also as he begins to drink his drink. Sara looking up from a short distance at Joshua, smiles. Then she moves over toward him. Joshua sees that Sara is one of the girls that has brought out the refreshments. As she approaches.

Sara: Is the apple cider good?

Joshua: (still slightly embarrassed) Yes, very…and nice and cold, thank you Sara.

Sara: I have something for you.

As she runs off toward the wagon which is alongside the road she passes the man that greeted Joshua early that morning when he came late. The man in an understanding glimpse breaks an understanding smile as she passes. At the wagon Sara retrieves a napkin-like package. Now holding it at her side she hurries back to where Joshua is sitting. Looking at him she places the napkin on the ground between them. Then she sits down with him.

Sara: Open it.

Joshua opens the napkin. There is a large muffin inside.

Sara: I noticed that you were missing from breakfast this morning. Thought you must have overslept. Thought you might be a little hungry by now.

Joshua: I'm starved... Thank you, Sara... Thank you, God! *(as he loses no time in getting to it)*

Sara gets up smiling and rejoins the other two girls as they collect the glasses and such, and put everything back into the cart at the side of the road. Sara comes back to Joshua to gather the napkin and his empty glass.

Sara: We've got to go back to school now.

Joshua: (smiling) Yeah, you've got to go back to school.

Sara: That's o.k...this winter while I'm packaging seeds for sale and cooking you'll be in school.

Joshua: All winter?

Sara: (she just smiles as she starts toward the cart... then turning back and looking over her shoulder for a moment) ... All winter...!

The scene fades as the three girls move off toward the village.

Chapter 10
Gathering the Ice

The snow is falling. It is dark and we can see the outline of the flakes as they continue to fall. The morning light is about to break as a flatbed open sleigh moves steadily upward toward the ridge. The smoke from the nostrils of the team of horses pulling it breathes into the chill of the oncoming day. In the still and quiet dark of the cold morning a group of seven Shaker men and boys sit upon an open flatbed sleigh as it moves slowly toward the lake near the ridge, where they will begin gathering the ice for their ice house and the hot summer which not so long ago was just here, and in not so long a time will be here once again. The outline of the northeastern pine can hardly be distinguished against the skyline. The sleigh continues being pulled ever and ever closer to the lighter sky on the opposite side of the ridge against the new horizon. The quiet change of the night into day is broken only by the crisp crunching sound of the sleigh blades steadily cutting through the crusted snow against the background sound of the horses' hooves as they penetrate the beauty of the frozen white cover.

Shaker Man: (sitting up front next to the driver and pointing) Take 'er over the ridge down to the right.

Driver: Good…follow the old road?

Shaker Man: Yes; think it's the best way. Less incline so

when we load up 'twont be so hard on these two *(pointing to the horses)*. A little bit 'round about, but I think better.

Driver: ...aye... *(turning to the others on the sleigh)*...'twont be long now.

The sleigh is now seen traversing a snow covered road winding amongst the pine. We are still slightly high up and are in what can only be described as a winter wonderland. Below we can see the clear area of a lake that is frozen over. The sleigh meanders down to the lakes edge and comes to a stop. Besides the men on board, the sleigh is loaded with hay, horse blankets, rope, wooden planks and various tools such as saws, augers for ice cutting and the like.

The first to dismount is the man sitting next to the driver. As he does so he walks around to the side of the sleigh.

Shaker Man: Everyone looks so cozy I hate to ask you to move. Just think though, when the blistering sun of summer comes we'll be ready for her. Josh... Eddie... you fetch us some wood and start a fine fire. Build it near those large rocks. They'll shelter it nicely from the wind.

Man on Board: Yeah, get that fire started boys. Here, take the lantern to borrow some flame.

With this the two boys jump off the sleigh. Eddie stretches and yawns as Josh adjusts the flaps on his cap. All the others dismount also. Everyone swings into action seeming to know exactly what to do, unloading the equipment and hay and blankets. Still others loose the horses and feed them some of the hay. They have come to the lake to cut ice for the ice house where they will store their meat and produce through the hot summer.

Shaker Man: Peter... Michael... Take the auger out there. Let's see how thick she is. First block is always the hardest.

The two men start to move toward an area of the lake where some men have already begun shoveling and sweeping the snow off of the ice. They have the ice auger with them. We can see the two boys building their fire in the background.

Joshua: (to Eddie) Let's hurry so we can get out there and see how thick she is.

Eddie: (excited) …Yeah…

They both hurry to pile and gather wood. They have also brought some dry wood with them from the sleigh. With some larger branches they brush and clear an area of snow near the rocks. The rocks are large and provide shelter. Then with the lantern they start a small fire. Looking up they can see that the men with the auger have reached their destination and are placing the auger.

Joshua: More wood!

Eddie and Josh hastily put more wood onto the fire that they have started. We can hear the crackling of the flames as the fire builds. One of the older men has made his way over to where the boys are busy hurriedly making their fire. Looking down at them he watches for a moment, looks at the pile of sticks and the fire, puts his hands on his hips and speaks.

Man: Everything in order; the sun, the earth, the stars, the snow and even our small fire. Everything in its place and everything in its order…Watch... *(he gestures to the boys)*

The older man, without haste, stoops down and untangles some twigs and branches. He then starts to rearrange them in order. Systematically he begins to build a fire.

Man: Now, let's bring over those larger logs. *(motioning to the boys)* The three bring over the larger wood and arrange them in a geometric square crisscrossing them until a fire is made in an orderly fashion.

Man: There…now we have a proper Shaker fire, everything in order.

The man takes off his gloves and faces his hands toward the growing flames.

Man: There now…that's much warmer. *(with a half smile on his face)* Why don't you boys go down to the ice and lend a hand. I'll keep my eye on the fire until you return.

The boys break out into an enthusiastic smile and dart toward the ice. As they run we can see the men working. As they approach, the auger suddenly plunges down.

Peter: Ho! We're through!…Looks to be just a little under two feet.

Chapter 11
The Good Room

Back in the village in the warm cooking room, or "good room", an overweight woman is opening the cast metal door of an oven. She snaps back quickly and puts her finger to her mouth. The door is very hot. She has burned her finger slightly. Making a sort of grunting sound she raises her thumb into the air. Sara, who is watching all of this, comes closer to the woman.

Sara: Did you burn your finger?

Woman: Just a bit.

Sara: Why are you holding it in the air?

Woman: So the Lord can make it better. If I hold it up He doesn't have so far to go.

Sara: Does God want some help?...I'll get the burn ointment!

Woman: God is the burn ointment! *(as she wraps a towel or rag around her hand and opens the metal oven door)* Come help me take these muffins out of the oven.

Little Sara, then wielding a large wooden pizza-like paddle with a short handle, slides it into the oven and removes a tray of muffins. She places the pan of muffins on a table top and repeats this procedure several times until there are four pans of muffins on the table top.

Woman: Thank you, Sara. Would you like to help me make another batch? Come, I'll teach you.

Sara is delighted and it is expressed in her face. The woman closes the oven door and moves over to an empty table. There are several bowls covered with cloth which seem to be bulging on the table top.

Woman: Now, let's get us some corn flour first. There from the sacks *(pointing to the sacks with her finger)*. Here's a wooden scoop. Fill this bowl. *(handing her a bowl and scoop)*

Sara does just as she is instructed returning with the bowl.

Woman: Now put the bowl here. *(pointing to the table)*... and the scoop there *(pointing to the shelf)*. Everything in its place, in order.

The woman gets a large bowl and a sieve.

Woman: I'll put the flour in the sieve and you sieve it into the bowl *(they finish the task)*. Now some salt...and some water... and molasses. O.k. now use the large wooden spoon and mix it. I'll get the muffin tins *(she gets the tins)*. Always lard up the tins... makes it easy to remove the muffins when they cool. Do you like cooking Sara?

Sara: Oh yes...it's fun. And it taste good, too.

Sara using the puffed part of her sleeve on her upper arm tilts her head to wipe off some perspiration from her brow.

Chapter 12
The First Block

With the wiping of the perspiration caused by the heat of the "good room" the scene flashes instantly back to the lake. In contrast we see the steam of the breath of the men as they are working at collecting ice. They are pushing a large block of ice across the frozen pond. They are close to the shore and the sleigh and fire can be seen. The old man is sitting near the fire. The missing block of ice can be seen as a large hole in the ice cover of the pond. Everyone is involved now in moving the large block of ice toward the sleigh which is near the edge of the lake. Some men are making a ramp of planks extending from the edge of the pond to the open part of the sleigh. Some push as others pull to get the block of ice situated on the planks and ready to be slid up onto the sleigh. Ropes are then put around the ice and attached to the horses. Together men and beast work until the ice is on the sleigh. As the first block is put upon the sleigh everyone cheers.

Everyone: Cheering.

The men now return to the hole in the ice. They take up a large saw and alternate taking turns cutting out the next block. The men return to the ice and the boys run over to the man at the fire. The fire is going full blast now. We can see the flicker of the flames reflect off of their faces. It is full daylight now.

Man: Welcome back. See you got the first one on board.

Eddie: Yeah, it was great Jonathan…'bout two feet thick.

Joshua: And very heavy. Had to pull it on with ropes… couldn't lift it. *(the old man just smiles)*

Man: Remember the first time I saw ice taken from the lake. Was about your age, I guess. Nature sure is a wonderful provider; year after year. We've been taking ice out of this lake for about seventy years now… every summer more water… every winter more ice, over and over. Nature's great…But now you've got the new ice house …makes me feel old.

Joshua: Jonathan, how come it doesn't just melt. I mean in the summer when it's hot how come it just doesn't melt?

Man: Well that's why we put earth around the ice house and make it out of such thick wood. That's why you have to cover the ice in the house with salt hay; to keep it from meltin' away. Oh, it does melt some, but slowly. It'll last the summer. When we go back you'll see that the ice is put on the top floor. The cold air is heavier than the heat and will keep the vegetables below the floor cold as it sinks….Fire sure does feel good...Hungry?

Joshua and Eddie: Yeah!

Man: Well it won't be long now. First blocks always the hardest.

They look toward the sleigh. Another block of ice is being loaded onto the sleigh.

Joshua: Let's go.

The two boys pop up and dart toward the sleigh.

Chapter 13
The First Loaf of Bread

The scene is back in the kitchen where Sara is taking tins of muffins out of the oven.

Woman: Now let's see how you did with your very first loaf of bread.

Sara reaches in with the wooden paddle and returns with a beautiful loaf of bread. Excited and proud she puts it on the table. The woman gives her a hug.

Woman: It's beautiful, Sara. *(as she hugs her)* It's the most beautiful loaf of bread I've ever seen.

All of the women in the kitchen smile and clap as Sara is both a bit embarrassed and delighted.

Chapter 14
Returning Home

The sleigh is fully loaded with ice. The horses are pulling it up the hill and over the crest. The ice has been covered with the horse blankets and everyone is sitting on top. The sun is bright now as they return home. The sleigh approaches and the doors to the ice house are opened. The men and boys off load the ice blocks into the upper chamber which is at ground level. After the ice has been placed into the ice house the Shaker men close the doors. Josh is there helping them secure the doors.

Shaker Man: There, that ought to hold 'er Josh. What do you think?

Joshua: Yep.

Shaker Man: We'll go out to the lake another day. I think one more trip ought to do it. What do you think?

Joshua: Yep.

Shaker Man: Well now, let's go to the house and see about some food...Sound good?

Joshua: Yep.

The man puts his hand on Joshes shoulder as they walk in the direction of the house. They enter and clean the snow off of their boots. They hang their coats upon the wooden pegs provided along the wall. There are the coats of the other men who were with them that have already entered the house. The wet shoes and boots of the other men are aligned beneath the coat pegs. They remove their shoes also and enter the room where the others are already seated. There is an air of joyousness about the room. The women are moving about serving the men that have arrived home. The man and Josh sit separately. The man goes to the head of the table while Josh finds an empty space next to Smitty.

Smitty: Beautiful day…beautiful day. Some day, ah Josh. Makes you come alive.

Joshua just smiles.

Smitty: Christmas time is almost here Josh. Another week …Another Christmas. Tell you what, how about you and I taking the small sleigh on Saturday and going on up to the ridge and getting us a tree for trimming. *(Smitty yells to everyone in the room)*….Hey, everybody listen up…On Saturday Josh and I are going up to bring down a tree for Christmas. So everyone come on over and help us trim it.

With this everyone cheers and talks excitedly. Josh smiles.

Chapter 15
The Tree

It is early evening now on the following Saturday. There are many more people now present in the same large room. The Christmas tree is completely trimmed. The children are eating cookies and playing. The older people are drinking cider and talking. Smitty interrupts the festivities.

Smitty: Everybody...*(pause)*...Everybody... It's time for the blessing. Elder Harris…..good sir, please bless our Shaker tree.

Everyone quiets down.

Elder Harris: (rises) May the Lord bless and keep you each and every one in the joy and peace of His love. As he protects you in the palm of his hand, holding you with his love, so may we remind ourselves of his holy goodness by that joy, and peace, and love that surrounds us here tonight. In this His season let us give thanks and praise his name. Glory to God our Father in Heaven, in the wonderful name of his son our Lord and risen Savior, Jesus Christ. Amen.

Everyone: Amen.

Sara: Let's sing some songs.

Smitty: O.k., o.k.….everyone make a circle around the tree…o.k., o.k.…everyone. *(Sara takes a place right next to Josh)* …Join hands…*(Sara and Josh join hands).*

They start singing Christmas songs. Josh and Sara smile at each other.

As the singing goes on Josh and Sara look more and more at each other. Their relationship begins in its infancy here on a more adult level. They have not only noticed each other, but acknowledge each other in a silent way. As they finish singing a lady elder approaches with a basket.

Lady Elder: In the basket are names. Each person take a name out of the basket as it is passed. Don't say whose name it is you have taken. *(The basket goes full circle)* Has everyone a name? Now for Christmas, in the spirit of giving, place that name upon a gift and place it under the tree between now and Christmas Day. Merry Christmas everybody.

Everyone: Merry Christmas.

Chapter 16
Christmas Church

At this point we fade, or blend, into Christmas Day. The scene is outside the Shaker Church. Sleighs are decorated and even the fence about the grounds has red bows on it. Bows of green and red decorate the windows. There are many people leaving the church. As was very often the case, when allowed, many of the townspeople would attend services at the Shaker worship. These people are now leaving and returning to town. The Shaker family however is walking to the main house and the Christmas tree. Soon everyone is around the tree again.

Elder Lady: Is everyone here? *(looking around)* O.k., let's give out the presents. Josh and Sara do us the honor of passing out the gifts.

The two go to the presents and start to hand them out. There are two gifts left. Josh picks up one and Sara the other. They straighten up, laugh and switch gifts. Each has picked up the others gift.

Everyone starts opening their gifts. There is much talking, oohs and ahhs.

Josh and Sara are still together. They look at each other. Josh speaks.

Josh: You first.

Sara: O.k.

She fumbles and finally gets her package open. Inside is a small and narrow felt like pouch. She opens the red ribbon that ties it and looks inside. Her eyes open wide.

Sara: Oh, Josh… a metal pen…oh Josh look…my own pen. There's a note attached…to Sara, Merry Christmas, Josh… Oh, Josh thank you, thank you…*(very excited she gives Josh a hug)*….Open yours, Josh.

He opens the soft paper package. Inside is a scarf and some hard candy.

Joshua: Thank you Sara…Thank you so very much.

He places the scarf around his neck and offers a piece of candy to Sara. Each of them, with a piece of candy in their mouth, reaches toward the other. Now joining hands they face each other.

Joshua: Merry Christmas, Sara.

Sara: Merry Christmas, Joshua.

With this Sara gives Josh a small kiss on the lips.

Chapter 17
The General Store

Joshua is now a grown young man. It is spring again and everything and everyone is coming to life. The earth and the entire universe with all of its inhabitants come out of hibernation to usher in the great and festive change in climate. The sun is warmer and the sky is filled with the activity and the chirping song of the darting birds as even they prepare to renew life once again in the cycle that God has provided us. We are in a small town near the Shaker village. The focus is a hardware and general store. It is just an old time hardware and general store toward the center of town laden down with wheelbarrows, and picks, and shovels, and open jars of candy, and yard goods folded and laid out on open flat tables. There are saddles and horse gear in abundance throughout the store. Blankets and flour, oil and lamps, everything that you could imagine is here in one place. Even the wooden plank sidewalk has barrels holding rakes and brooms and the like sitting on it, out for sale in front of the "Old Hardware and General Store". This is the common meeting ground for all the area. The street is busy that afternoon as the flatback buckboard makes its way through the ruts and furrows of the dusty main street. On top is Smitty and Joshua as they come to town bumping, and talking and laughing. As they come to a full stop in front of the store, Joshua jumps down off of his seat and runs around to the front of the wagon. While Josh is hitching the horses up to the hitching rail Smitty is dismounting.

He calls to Josh.

Smitty: Josh, you go in and pick up the salt and threads. I'm going to take a walk down to the livery, see how John is doing. Maybe even talk a little shop. Pick me up when you're finished.

Josh acknowledges Smitty and starts toward the store. Inside of the store Belle and Tom are looking over some clothing in the back part of the store as Josh enters the store. Belle looks up and sees Joshua. She simply lights up. Immediately starting toward him she calls out.

Belle: Joshua! *(now near to him she reaches out and gives him an enormous hug)* Child, where have you been hiding? Look at you. You're all grow'd up.

Joshua is very happy and hugs Belle, spinning her around. Tom has made his way over also.

Joshua: *(while exchanging her hug)* Aunt Belle. *(Then reaching out to take the hand of Tom)* Tom, how are you?

Tom: Hey boy, where have you been hiding? When you coming out visiting with Tom and Belle?

Joshua: *(obviously delighted to see them)* Been real busy on the farm, and in school, and helping Smitty.

Belle: Too busy to come out on Sunday afternoon and have some of Belle's apple pie, and ham and 'tatters?

Joshua: Nope. Never be that busy.

Belle is absolutely delighted.

Tom: What 'cha in town for today?

Joshua: Well, Smitty and I came to trade for some salt and thread for the community. Smitty is down at the livery stable talking to John. Have to pick him up in a little bit.

Shopkeeper: Josh, got your usual order of salt and thread up front. Whenever you're ready.

Tom and Josh move to the front of the store together. Josh tries to lift the heavy sack of salt but finds it a little difficult. Tom lends a helping hand and the two followed by Belle move the supplies out to the wagon. There Tom helps Josh put the salt on board. Then they walk together to the driver's side. Josh is about to mount up when he realizes that he forgot to say goodbye to Belle. He walks over to her and gives her a believer's kiss *(a kiss on the cheek)* and a great big hug. After this he returns to the driver's seat. Tom and Belle remain to see him off.

Tom: See you on Sunday, 'bout twelve. Don't eat no breakfast now. Belle be waiting with enough food to fill 'bout twelve of you.

Joshua, as he pulls away.

Joshua: 'Bye, Belle...'Bye, Tom...See you on Sunday... Thank you ...Bless...

Tom is in the street and Belle is upon the wooden sidewalk facing the wagon as it makes its way toward the opposite side of town and to the livery. Tom and Belle make their way to re-enter the store.

The wagon soon approaches the livery where Smitty and John are outside talking. Smitty and his friend are having a good time. Smitty is seated on a box.

Smitty: Looks like my ride is here. See you in a month or so, John. *(as he starts to board the wagon)*... Bless now.

As they drive off, Smitty talks to Josh.

Smitty: See you got the salt and thread.

Joshua: Yes…Saw Tom and Belle. Tom helped me load it. Saw them in the store. They invited me out on Sunday. Think it will be alright?

Smitty: Sure, they brought you to the Elders. You and me coming to town every once in a while is about as much going out as we get to do. It'll do you good to do some visiting once in a while. People is people… I like people….All people are in the same boat Josh…Just we all pulling on different oars.

With this Smitty starts singing his favorite Shaker song, as Josh listens.

Smitty: Our tools are kind and gentle words …Our shop is in the heart…And here we manufacture peace …That we may such impart…Come life, Shaker life! Come life eternal!...Come life, Shaker life! Come life eternal!

Chapter 18
Apple Picking

The scene shifts to the early fall and the beautiful, full apple orchards near the Shaker village. The air is cool, crisp and clean, and the smell of fresh fall apples is in the air.

The young men of the village have gathered under the direction of one of the Elders, and apple picking, one of the funnest chores, is about to begin.

Elder: Come on boys, let's get some apples.

They all talk and smile with enthusiasm as they make their way into the orchards, which are overflowing with ripe, red apples.

The boys throw up the ladders against the trees and start picking the apples; some while standing on the ladders, some while standing on the lower branches heavy with abundant fruit, some catching the ripe fresh bounty in sheets which are spread on the ground beneath the trees as they fall to the earth, and still others by just climbing on the tree limbs, not well accepted by the Elder, but just as fun, and the Elder just smiles faintly, understandingly, as if as a boy he had done the same thing.

Eddie: What do you think, Josh?

Joshua: I think it's great…*(he bites into an apple)*…enough apples here for a long time.

Eddie: …And the pies… *(says Eddie looking at the apples they have collected in the bags already).* This is going to be one happy person when Sara and the women gets to bakin' pies with these apples.

Joshua and Eddie enjoy a well-deserved laugh.

After several hours of picking, the Elder, fully proud, announces to the group.

Elder: O.k. that should do it. We don't take more than we need right now and we can come back for more later.

They start to load the apples onto the cart.

Elder: That's good Josh. *(says the elder approaching the boys who have surrounded themselves with baskets of apples)*…….Now thank the tree……..

Joshua: How do you do that?

Elder: Put your hand on the tree…*(he places his hand on the trunk of the tree)*…and say thank you. After all it gave us a wonderful gift, a supply of God's good fruit that he made for us…and God, don't forget to thank God, after all, it's His tree.

Joshua puts his hand on the trunk of the tree.

Joshua: Thank you tree.

Elder: …and God…

Joshua: …and God…

The Elder smiles and turns to the group.

Elder: O.k. gentlemen let's go home and get these apples to the women.

The young men get into the cart and start back to the village.

Chapter 19
The Church

The scene has changed, many years have passed. It is a cool spring morning. There is a treed lane. As we travel along this picture perfect lane we come to a white building at the turn in the road. It is the Shaker Church. As we approach, we can hear, even though we have not yet entered into the church, that a service is in progress. There is much stomping and singing going on as we enter through the front doors. There with his arms raised is the elder preacher totally worked up, just finishing his service. And as the congregation continue to dance and sing, above it all we can hear him as he is obviously ending his sermon.

Elder Preacher: (loud and with fire above the march like dancing and singing of the congregation) And we know…..

Congregation: And we know…

Elder Preacher: And we believe…

Congregation: And we believe…

Elder Preacher: That our brethren! *(close up of his sweating face)*

Congregation: Yes Lord… *(close up of men and women as they answer)*

Elder Preacher: And our sisters… *(close up of preacher's face)*

Congregation: Oh yes Lord… *(close up of woman's face)*

The congregation is getting more and more worked up as more and more of the congregation enter into the ceremony of the service. There is a young girl, about eighteen, in the back pew of the church. Her face is nervous and she is not entering into the excitement of the moment. The preacher continues. She (the girl) glances to the window, then back again to him. Removing a small handkerchief from her sleeve she wipes small tears from her eyes. She is a true Shaker girl whose rose colored cheeks and pure white skin is set by the beauty of her soft brown hair. The more the congregation continues the more nervous she becomes.

Elder Preacher: And even those children once departed…

Congregation: Oh yes…yes Lord… *(really into it)*

Elder Preacher: Even now… *(close up)*

Congregation: Even now…

Elder Preacher: Are showering down gifts and blessings… Yes mighty gifts and blessings…

Congregation: Mighty blessings.

Elder Preacher: From Heaven up above…

Congregation: (crazy and screaming) Up above.

Elder Preacher: Down on us today…

Congregation: Yeah, Lord.

Elder Preacher: For us to gather …In our hearts…

Congregation: In our hearts.

Elder Preacher: In our souls…

Congregation: Our souls.

Elder Preacher: In our minds…

Congregation: Yes Lord.

At this point the Shakers are all up with the exception of our girl in the last row. They are now fully frantic, marching with their arms fully extended and bending them at the elbow toward themselves as if to catch the blessings from above and gather them onto themselves. As they move in an almost march like dance they stomp their feet. All of the women are on one side of the room, and all of the men are on the other side of the room. They march and stomp toward each other but never cross the aisle in the center of the church which separates them from each other. The place is frantic.

Elder Preacher: Forever…

Congregation: Yes Lord.

Elder Preacher: And ever…

Congregation: Ever.

Elder Preacher: Amen.

Congregation: Amen.

The dancing is a frenzy now as the preacher yells out above it all, as he starts to sit and reside over them.

Elder Preacher: Now shake brethren…and sistren…Shake off all your sins.

With this the entire congregation starts to shake. Further and further, deeper and deeper into a frenzied shake. They are now absolutely wild.

We see the bench where the girl was seated in the back row. The seat is empty but the door near the place where she sat is open. In the middle of all of the commotion she has left the church. We look toward the open window that she looked toward earlier. There running across a sunlit field clinging to her simple white and greyish blue dress is our beautiful Shaker girl. She makes her way across the field to a barn. The doors of the barn are open. She enters through the open barn doors and stops in the inner shade of the barn for a moment. There, a bearded stoic looking young man is putting some small pieces of furniture onto a wagon along with some personal belongings. It is a small wagon of Shaker design drawn by only one beautiful black horse. He is finishing tying on the last piece. She runs to him just as he finishes and looks up. Taking her into his arms and smiling he twirls her, and without one word lifts her into the seat of the wagon. He then jumps up into his seat. Releasing the break and gently moving the reins he starts the horse and wagon moving forward. He looks in a loving way over to her as they leave the barn. She smiles.

Joshua: I love you too much not to want to have a family and spend the rest of my life with you.

Sara: And I with you, Josh.

Joshua: I just can't agree with the belief in celibacy that our people follow. I look at you and I know one thing, "procreation sure beats no creation". Sara, when God made you he sure knew what he was doing.

Sara then just moves over toward him and smiles. He puts his arm around her as they continue to drive away from the church.

The wagon continues to travel throughout the day. Sara at one point reaches behind the seat and retrieves a folded napkin with something in it. She gives it to Josh, and he opens it. Inside is a freshly baked muffin. He throws his head back as he laughs. Then he hugs her tight, and eats the muffin. Throughout the evening and into the night the wagon moves along. The trees and sunlit road now give way to the shadows of the later day. As the moon rises and the sun sinks onto the beautiful skyline beyond the mountains, Sara takes a quilt and covers herself extending it to cover Josh also. The moonlit night is actually light enough to see the way. Then with a yawn the young lady makes herself comfortable against her driver husband and goes off to sleep as the monotonous rhythm of the horse's hoofs can be heard even more clearly now in the still of the night. Then Josh looks down at his young bride and whispers in a low voice so as not to wake her.

Joshua: Sara….My Sara. *(as he hugs and makes her more comfortable)*

She stirs closer to him as she remains asleep. The night grows deeper and the darkness more intense as the steady clomping of the horse can still be heard. Now in the still of the night she sleeps. For a short time the night and the methodic sound of the hoofs and of the horse's breathing continue. Then as the sounds of the night lessen so also does the light of the new day invade the quietness of the passing night, and birth is given to the new light of the new day. We focus on Joshua as he drives his wagon with his new bride aboard into the brighter sunlit morning, and into the heat of the afternoon. Sara is awake now. She speaks to Josh.

Sara: Josh, you have been driving a long time now. You must be tired. And the horse…I'm sure he could use a rest?

Joshua: And Sara? Could she use a rest also?

Sara smiles up at Josh.

Sara: Only if you want to stop, Josh.

Joshua: Ahead there's a field that looks mighty refreshing.

Sara: Thank you, Josh.

She moves over and rests her head against his arm. Josh just looks down.

Joshua: The rest will do us both good…*(pause)*…me and the horse, that is.

Sara: And I brought along some fine food for us for just such an occasion…*(pause)* …well, for me and the horse.

He laughs as the wagon turns to the side of the road and then off into the field. There under the shade of a large chestnut tree they dismount. Josh sets the horse loose from the wagon and tethers him by a long rope to the tree. Then in the shade of the tree he takes off his hat, wipes his brow, falls to his knees, gives thanks, and then lays stretched out upon the cool green grass. As he does these things Sara has been getting some things out of the wagon. She is obviously getting something for them to eat. However, by the time she gets to Josh he is fast asleep in the shade. Sara abandons the food and comforts Joshua by removing his hat from his hand and puts some clothing beneath his head for a pillow. Then she sits beside him and strokes his hair.

Sara: (softly in a whisper and with loving compassion) Thank you for stopping, Joshua. I was very tired.

She gently smiles at him as he sleeps.

Chapter 20
The Mouse

It is an old wooden house as near to ruin as a house can get without being in ruin. On the front porch is a grizzly old man with a wooden peg leg. He is stomping about the front porch with a broom half yelling at something as he moves about.

Old Man: Come out here and stand up like a man you four legged moocher. *(waving the broom)* I'll teach you to have more respect for the house I built…and you took over. You two eared fuzzy creep, I'll teach you some manners.

With this a small field mouse shoots past him. He whirls on his peg leg and swings the broom like a golf club in the direction that the mouse ran, missing him completely and landing on his butt, as the only result of his effort.

Old Man: (waving the broom in one hand) I'll get you for this. *(putting the broom down and totally exasperated)* …This is war!... *(lifting himself up)* Eat my corn…open my sack of flour…steal my sugar!

Now he is up. He throws open the screen door and goes inside. The mouse comes out of a little hole as if to say "what's going on?" The screen door opens again and the old man reappears carrying an old musket. Just as he is about to engage in phase two of his attack on the enemy he looks up and pauses.

From the porch we see a one horse wagon on the not too distant horizon. We can make out that it is Joshua and Sara. The old man looks squinting in the sunlight as he moves off of the porch toward the oncoming wagon as if to get a better look.

Old Man: (under his breath) Now who in tarnation? *(looking back in the direction of the mouse)* I'll deal with you later. *(the mouse retreats to his hole)*

The wagon approaches. Both Sara and Joshua wave to the old man. He in turn waves back with the gun. Soon the wagon is entering onto the property. Josh pulls the horse up to a halt. He then dismounts and approaches the old fellow.

Old Man: Howdy.

Joshua: Good morning and God's blessings to you sir.

Josh reaches out and offers his hand in friendship. The old man shakes Joshes hand.

Old Man: What can I do for you young fella?

Joshua: Well, to tell you the truth my wife and I are traveling and I was wondering if there might be an inn nearby. The light will be growing short soon and we could sure use a good night's rest.

Old Man: Put your horse 'round back. There's some oats in the sack out back. Give 'em some…*(under his breath as he turns toward the house)*…lessen my buddy ate 'em all. Then you and the misses come on inside. Ain't no inn here 'bouts.. In fact ain't nothin' here 'bouts…*(under his breath)*…'ceptin my little buddy… and I'm about to change that.

Joshua: Hunting?

Old Man: Oh…? Oh, the gun…It can wait.

Joshua moves the horse and wagon to the side of the house and then unhitches the horse from the wagon. He leads the animal around to the back of the house. There in the rear of the house stands an old dilapidated lean-to with room enough in it for just two horses. The shelter has light coming through the roof. There is a donkey in one half of the shelter. Joshua brings his horse to the lean-to. There in the corner is a bin and inside the bin is a bag of oats. He reaches into the bin and takes several handfuls of grain for his horse. Then spilling the oats into a pail held by a nail on the wall he repeats the procedure several times. After the pail is half full he brings it over to the horse. With that accomplished he puts his hands on his hips and looks around the lean-to. Just shaking his head slightly he gives half a smile, nods his head yes, puts his hand to his chin and supports the elbow at his stomach with the other hand. He waits for a moment as if to be figuring, and then turns and leaves.

Later that evening Joshua and Sara retire to bed. There is just enough moonlight entering the room so that we can see the shine of the evening on their faces. They are awake side by side under a quilt, talking in a slow, half talk, half whisper.

Sara: The old man is very nice and quite "piculiar", Josh. What do you think?

Joshua: I think he is one of God's people and I thank him for showing us this hospitality. He is truly very nice …and very "piculiar".

Sara: Good night my Joshua.

With this Sara comes to Joshua putting her head upon his chest, near his shoulder. There is a short pause, then Joshua speaks.

Joshua: You know, Sara, in Sunday service I could never take my eyes off of you. You were the most beautiful thing I think I'd ever seen, you were even more beautiful than some of the horses Smitty showed me.

Sara hits him with a pillow. They both laugh.

Joshua: (as the light fades) Good night my Sara.

Chapter 21
A New Morning

It is morning now and the light of the new day begins to fill the room where Josh and Sara had fallen asleep. She is half asleep and half awake. We can hear in the background the pounding of a hammer driving nails and the occasional sound of a saw. Sara sits up in bed realizing that Joshua is not there. Then hearing the hammer she surmises that it is Joshua who must be at the other end of the noise. She turns to get up. There sitting at the foot of the bed on the footboard watching her is the mouse. Sara leaves the bed in one bounding motion and ascends up onto a chair. Putting her hand over her mouth she muffles a scream.

Sara: Schoo…..Schoo…..Get away from here.

She picks up the pillow from the bed and throws it at the mouse. It goes sailing over the creatures head. The mouse turns and cocks his head looking right at Sara as if to say, "Is everyone crazy around here. I just came to say good morning." He then jumps down off of the bed onto the floor and darts away. Sara starts down off of the chair.

Outside the house, the lean-to is looking a little better now. Once outside the house we can see both the lean-to as well as the house. It seems that Joshua was up very early repairing holes and supports. It is clean inside and out. As he puts some finishing touches on it, both Sara and the old man come out of the house and make their way toward Joshua. As they do Joshua comes down off of the roof.

Joshua: What do you think?

Old Man: Well I'll be! The holes are gone. Thank you sonny…Thank you very much. See with this here captain's leg, this old pirate can't hardly make it up onto the roof any more. I do thank you.

Joshua: No it's I who should be thanking you for taking my wife and me into your home.

Old Man: Are you kidding. It's good just having folks 'round.

Joshua: Speaking of which Sara. We had better be getting on our way.

Old Man: Not so fast. Not 'till you've had some of my vittles. Refuse to let you start on an empty stomach.

They go in to breakfast.

Chapter 22
A Quiet Afternoon on the Lake

After breakfast Joshua and Sara thank the old man, pack their wagon, and start on their way again. It isn't long before they are out of sight.

It is a beautiful day and the old man, feeling pretty good, decides to go fishing.

The water on the pond is very smooth this day. In fact the "V" shaped design made by the family of mallards swimming on its surface spreads quietly from their rear feathers to the water's edge. There on the fringe of the pond is our old friend with his peg leg looking like some old retired pirate. Placing his fishing pole and a pair of oars into a small row boat he maneuvers to free it from the shore where it has been lodged. Now entering the boat he pushes it off using one of the oars for that purpose. Finally adrift he settles himself onto the plank seat and sets the oars into position. Now pulling on the oars he maneuvers the craft toward the center of the pond. The boat, like the mallards who seemed unconcerned by this, makes its mark upon the glass-like water spreading its after wake like some watery fan behind it as it goes. Now nearing his watery destination he pulls the oars into the boat and takes out his pipe. After lighting it, he looks to the sky first and then to his peaceful surroundings. Pleased with the day and his surroundings he grunts his approval and baits the hook of the fishing pole beside him. A fish jumps out of the water not far from the boat.

Old Man: Ha...Ha...Looks like a big one just waiting to be caught.

He sighs and settles back for a relaxed day of fishing.

Old Man: What a beautiful day. Quiet, no one to disturb a man's soul.

He cast his line out to where the fish had jumped.

Old Man: Come on little fishy, bite the bait. Hee, hee... if that stupid mouse could only see me now. *(sigh)* ...Alone at last and no one to bother me.

Then he settles back even more, semi-reclining in the bow of the boat, his bottom on the deck and his legs draped over the seat as his head rests in the point of the bow.

Soon the sun starts to lull him to sleep. There in a semi-sleep, fully relaxed he drifts, lulled by the ever gentle movement of an occasional breeze against the side of the row boat.

A fly disturbs him momentarily and he shushes it away from his face still half awake and half asleep.

Squeaky the Mouse: Squeak........ squeak, squeak.

The mouse jumps up onto the seat as if purposely trying to get the old timers attention.

Squeaky the Mouse: (again) Squeak.

The mouse watches the old man..."hmmm...No reaction."

Squeaky the Mouse: (now very loud) SQUEAK!!!!!!!

One eye pops open, then two. Now wide eyed the old man looks eye to eye with the mouse who stretches in defiance.

Old Man: No!....Not you!...Not here!...Not now!...No,No,No,No.

Rags

I'll get you. You're finally gonna get it; right here *(as he struggles to get up)*, right now!

As he struggles the fishing pole goes over the side. As it does it is dragged through the water. The fish that the old man wanted to catch has taken the bait, but now drags the pole away from the boat.

Old Man: (looking at the pole being dragged away) Oh, no! Now you're gonna die, you vermin. You wasn't invited on this here fishing trip.

Now fully on his feet he approaches the mouse. There is anger in his eyes as he slowly approaches the mouse.

Old Man: This is it. Your last day. This is the last time, the last straw. This is it!

The mouse drops down and retreats to the back of the boat.

Old Man: (slowly following and seemingly cornering the mouse) Now with this here old peg leg of mine I'm going to grind you into oblivion. Once and for all you're going to be gone.

The old man raises his peg leg as he looks the mouse right in the eye. The mouse looks back. Then with a sudden thrust the old man stamps his leg down with a thunderous force. While doing it he shouts.

Old Man: Finally! At last! I got you now.

The old man continues to push harder and harder.

Then from the other end of the boat, behind the old man, we hear a noise.

Squeaky the Mouse: (at the other end of the boat) Squeak.

The old man turns toward the squeak, realizing he has missed the mouse. But he is stuck. His peg leg has penetrated the bottom of the boat. Pulling all the harder because of his rage he frees his wooden leg. However in the process a board comes loose from the bottom of the boats floor. He looks back. Water begins to pour into the boat.

Old Man: Oh shit.

The boat now starts to sink faster and faster.

Soon the old man is up to his chest in water. The mouse is safely floating toward the shore on a floating oar. The ducks come floating by as if nothing has happened. The old man starts shouting.

Old Man: I'll get you yet... I'll get you...You won't get away...Vermin...I'll get you!

In the distance we hear a reply.

Squeaky the Mouse: Squeak.

Chapter 23
A New Life

Joshua and Sara, and the wagon packed with their belongings, are on the road again.

Sara: Joshua, where are we going?

Joshua: Springfield.

Sara: What's in Springfield?

Joshua: (pause) ….Springfield…. *(making a joke)*

Sara: Oh, that's very good. Now that you've filled me in on all the details is there anything else I should know?

Joshua: Yes.

Sara: Yes what?

Joshua: Yes I love you. Here, there, in the air…even in Springfield. I'll still love you… so…what else is there to know about it.

Sara: Oh……..men.

It isn't long before the wagon, Sara, and Joshua are approaching a town. We can see a large sign hanging from a tree limb near the road. It is a wooden sign and burned into it in large letters is the word Springfield. We see the sign as if it were mounted on the back of the wagon constantly bumping according to the pots and grooves in the dirt road beneath the hard round spoked wheels of the wagons planks. We focus on the sign until it passes. Soon the sign is passed and as the wagon makes its way down the center street of the town and past the treed homes and small shops, Sara speaks.

Sara: Is this to be our new home, Josh?

There is some degree of excitement in her voice as the town seems amiable and nice.

Joshua: I am believing that it is to be our new home, Sara.

Sara: Oh look Josh, a dress shop. And look in the window there are some clothes made at the village. Shall we stop Joshua, please?

Joshua: In a moment. First I want to find a livery for my horse, then a place for us, and then a job. Pray on it. I will also. And if two ask the same thing in His name that establishes it.

As the wagon continues down the main street it approaches the main intersection of the town. There are people moving about. Joshua pulls up to the crossroads undecided as to which direction to take. He stops and appraises the situation. To the right it is active with people going about their business. As he looks to the left he is astonished. His face lights up into a big smile. There, right there in Springfield, is the "Pharmacy and Seed Wagon" from the village heading directly toward him, a sort of Shaker traveling herb shop. With some excitement he starts his wagon moving across the intersection and to the left. Approaching the seed wagon now on the opposite side of the street he pulls up to a halt, as does the driver of the other Shaker wagon, who has obviously recognized Joshua.

Joshua: Eddie!

He hurriedly dismounts and goes across to greet his friend who also has pulled to the side of the road and has dismounted and who is very happy to see Joshua.

Joshua: (as he walks up to Eddie and hugs him. Sara is there also now) Eddie, how are you? What a surprise to see you here.

Eddie: I'm fine Josh. And you Joshua, how are you? Sara! *(Sara and Eddie hug and exchange a believer's kiss)* Sara, how are you? Is he treating you good, Sara?

Sara: I'm fine Eddie. And I don't know how he's treating me yet. We haven't really had a chance to settle anywhere as of yet. However, I guess I'll keep him 'till I find out.

Eddie: Joshua…Sara, what are you doing here?

Joshua: Well, to tell you the truth Eddie, we were thinking and actually believing that we might take up and live our lives together here in Springfield.

Eddie: It's a good town Joshua. It has a good future what with the railroad and all.

Joshua: I see the village is venturing out further and further *(referring to the Pharmacy and Seed Wagon)*. How's business?

Eddie: Excellent. Sales out here are way up, we are doing very well. The people here seem to especially like our product. I sell a lot of seed for homes as well as for the farmers. And our rheumatism and cough elixirs are very famous here. *(Eddie continues)* And you Joshua, where will you work? Where will you live?

Joshua: As yet I do not have an answer to these questions. Only questions myself. But I trust God for my sufficiency.

Eddie: Follow me. I'll turn around…follow me.

With this Eddie jumps back up into his seed wagon and Josh and Sara cross back over to their wagon and get back on board. Eddie turns his wagon around and as he passes Joshua he motions with a wave of his arm for Joshua to follow him. The wagons move in single file down the street 'till they reach the edge of town. Then the first wagon enters a drive between the stone walls of what is the home of a person of obvious wealth. They continue up the drive and come face to face with what can only be described as a northern plantation. There at the entrance Eddie pulls his wagon up to a halt. Joshua follows suit. Both young men get down from their wagons and meet.

Joshua: What is this place, Eddie?

Eddie: It belongs to Alexander Beaumont Brown. Do you remember who he is?

Joshua: No.

Eddie: Good. He is a very old and very wealthy entrepreneur who was instrumental in bringing the railroad to this place. He was originally in the foundry business. What's more important is that he is one of my best customers and in visiting with him on my trips here we have talked many times. He knows of our way of life, and actually I have already on occasion mentioned you to him. I've told him how you are my friend and how gifted you were in mechanicals. Come let's talk with him.

The three approach the large house together. They make their way up the front steps to the large front door. There beneath the white portico, the three stand beside the long white columns which reach to the second story. Eddie approaches the door without hesitation and uses the large brass knocker, the sound of which resounds in the hollowness of the vestibule behind. Moments pass and the door opens. There to greet them is a black servant named Alfred. He recognizes Eddie at once. It is evident that Eddie has been here before.

Alfred: Mr. Eddie, sir.

Eddie: Alfred, how are you?

Alfred: I'm just fine Mr. Eddie. Hope you are fine also, Mr. Eddie. Come in …come inside.

Eddie: Thank you, Alfred. Alfred, is Mr. Brown available, I'd like him to meet someone. Alfred this is Joshua and his wife Sara.

Alfred: Pleased to meet you Mr. Joshua…Miss Sara.

Joshua: My pleasure.

Sara: Alfred. *(greeting him)*

Alfred: Come make yourselves comfortable. I'll get Mr. Brown. He's happy to receive guests.

Mr. Brown: Alfred, who is it? *(he calls from a distance)*

Alfred: Mr. Brown, sir. I was coming to get you. Guests, sir, Mr. Eddie and his friends, Mr. Joshua and Miss Sara.

By this time Mr. Brown has entered the room. Mr. Brown is an elderly gentleman. In fact he is quite old but a bit distinguished. He first walks over to Eddie and greets him as one would an old friend.

Mr. Brown: Eddie, what a pleasant surprise. What brings you back at this time?

Eddie: To be honest sir, my two best friends, Joshua *(gesturing in his direction)*, and his most beautiful wife Sara.

Mr. Brown: Joshua…*(reaching out his hand to shake Joshua's hand)*, Sa..ra…*(pause)*…Sara, Sara…Excuse me… It's just that for a moment I saw my first wife. She…well…she looked, that is for the moment you looked quite like she used to. That is before she passed.

Sara: I'm sorry.

Mr. Brown: No don't be…thank you. That was a long time ago. Her name was Sara also…and like you she was quite beautiful. *(he continues)* Please, please sit down. Make yourselves comfortable. Tell me Joshua, Sara…What brings you to these parts?

Eddie: Well sir, that's why, actually I brought them to meet you. You see, Josh and Sara are considering settling in these parts and I thought they should meet you.

Mr. Brown: Thank you, Eddie. That was quite thoughtful of you. Are they from your village?

Eddie: Yes sir, but it's more than that. Do you remember about a year or so ago when you needed a part made for the railroad. And no one could make it. Remember I took it to the village and had it made for you?

Mr. Brown: Yes of course, a beautiful piece of work. That kind of workmanship is hard to come by now a days.

Eddie: Well, Josh here made that part for you.

Mr. Brown: Excellent! I want to thank you personally. It helped us no end. You see I personally believe that the railroad will have a great future in our country. I'm a businessman and a businessman must have vision. You must be able to see past today and build toward the future. The railroad to me is that future and I believe those that see it now and take advantage of what they see will be the future of all transportation in the near future. One day I envision all of the timber, and coal, and livestock and whatever product there is, being shipped to and fro across the entire face of this great country of ours. And me, well I just want to be a part of it. *(he pauses turning to Sara)* I'm sorry…Sara would you like some tea? Josh, Eddie, some cider, or coffee? I know you don't indulge, but I do occasionally… Alfred, ask Emily to make some nice tea for our guests. And Alfred bring us our usual brandy. You and I must not forget to toast today.

Alfred leaves to do as Mr. Brown has said. After he leaves

Mr. Brown speaks once more. This time a little softer as if to be a little more secretive and thereby justifying what he will say next.

Mr. Brown: Alfred and I have been together a long time now, and each day at about this time he and I toast the day with a brandy. It's become our own tradition, and it keeps the old heart pumping.

Sara: May I help, please?

Mr. Brown: Of course Sara, if you wish. Alfred will show you where the kitchen is and he will introduce you to Emily.

Mr. Brown waits and looks over the back of his chair as Alfred and Sara leave. He waits and watches until he is sure that they are out of hearing range. Then he turns back to Eddie and Josh and slaps his knee and laughs at the same time.

Mr. Brown: Eddie, I got bad news, and I got good news. Do you remember that old widow that used to nag me to death trying to convince me that I should marry her. Well this winter she fell deathly ill. We all knew that if we didn't do something she was bound to pass. She was about as ill as you can get… and that's the bad news. Do you remember all the remedies I purchased from you last year? Well we knew without them she wouldn't stand a chance. So we ministered them to her. And this is the good news… They didn't work! *(slaps his knee again)*

Eddie and Josh just look at each other as Mr. Brown could care less as he laughs himself silly.

Mr. Brown: (continues) I'm a man of few words when it comes to business. The braking systems on these trains are horrible. And in the future I can foresee the speeds of the railroads increasing to unheard of numbers; forty, even fifty miles per hour. The need for better braking systems will increase as the need for railroads increases. I'm betting on it. I want to create the company that will supply all of the trains with the best darn braking systems they can buy. And I want them to have to buy it from me. Josh, I want you to create that shop and run it for me. In a word, will you take on the challenge…yes or no..?

Joshua: Yes!

Joshua and Eddie and Mr. Brown shake hands as Eddie and Joshua are outwardly pleased.

Mr. Brown: Well, son. You have got yourself a job. I guess you're wondering why I'm doing this at all. I mean I'm so old now that I'll never see the final result of what I've started here today. And Lord knows I don't need the money. Couldn't spend what I have from now 'till I cash in all my chips. Well, let me tell you something, Josh. It's very much like an artist. I mean, why does an artist paint a picture and then after it's created or made, sell it, or give it away. Because there are two joys…one in creating…the other in the enjoyment of what has been created. I know I'll never live long enough to enjoy the second joy, but I want an opportunity to share the first with you.

The others now return to the room. Emily, Alfred and Sara bring the refreshments. Everyone takes their tea, or cider, or brandy.

Eddie: A toast… to Josh and Sara in their new place… to Joshua's new job… to Mr. Brown's continued health and success…And to all that is good from God…Bless.

All: (mixed voices) Cheers, God bless.

Mr. Brown: (after they have started drinking) Speaking of a place to live….Josh, Sara, I own several small houses in town. I want you to be my guests in one for several weeks until you get your bearings. Then if you like it there you may stay. It's all part of the package. Joshua, I promise you this. That if you develop this brake system for me and develop this company, when I pass on to that big factory in the sky, I'll will the entire operation to you. I promise.

The next scene is outside of Mr. Brown's house. We are looking at the front door. It opens and Joshua, Eddie and Sara exit with Alfred. They congregate on the front porch for a moment and then as they start down the front steps we pick up their conversation. Eddie and Josh stop and are shaking hands.

Joshua: Eddie, I don't know how to thank you.

Eddie: No need. We're all the same family, right… Brothers in Christ.

Sara: (as she gives Eddie a big hug) And sisters, too.

Eddie: And sisters, too. Well… *(pause)* …I guess it's time for me to be heading back.

Joshua: Thanks again, Eddie. *(as he shakes his hand).* Say hello to everyone back home at the village. Tell Smitty about my new job. He'll be real proud.

Sara: 'Bye Eddie, God bless.

Eddie: (as he gets up onto his wagon and starts to drive off) I'll be back this way soon. See you all then.

Joshua, Sara, Alfred: (in unison) 'Bye Eddie…Bless.

Alfred: Well, Mr. Joshua and Miss Sara, are you ready to go to your new home? It ain't much, but it ain't far either.

Joshua: Alfred, we're very thankful.

Sara: Very thankful.

Alfred: I'll go 'round back and get my horse. Be only a minute, then you can follow me to the house. I'll help you get settled in.

Rags

Sara: Thank you, Alfred.

Joshua and Sara get in their wagon and follow Alfred, who leads the way on his horse.

Following this we see Alfred on his horse leaving the two on the front yard of a small cottage type house. It is dusk and the light of this day is fast giving way to the oncoming night. It is evident at this point that they have moved into the house with the help of Alfred who is now leaving. The first sounds of evening are now first becoming evident. There is a light in the house which shows through the window. Josh and Sara turn and move toward the front steps. Ascending the three wooden steps they sit on the top step. Sara then moves closer to Joshua. He looks comfortingly upon her and reaches his arm out toward her. She moves closer to him resting against his chest.

Joshua: Sara, you've had quite a day.

Sara: Yawns…Oh, I'm sorry Josh

Joshua: You have to be exhausted, Sara.

Sara has fallen asleep against Joshua. She does not answer. They just sit still and quiet as the darkness of the cool night envelopes them. The darkness grows deeper as the sounds of crickets and the night increase in magnitude. Only the moon and the light from the window enable us to still see the figures there on the steps. There is a very large and clear night sky now filled with stars and a big soft yellow moon. The sky looks like a big birthday cake and each star a candle upon it. Soon the sky starts to lighten upon the horizon as the sun starts to rise, and one by one the candles from the previous night disappear.

Chapter 24
Our Hero Rags

Soon the sun is out in full array as the scene shifts to a new time and a new place. There in the brightness of the new morning is our hero, looking like a "bum", sleeping on a park bench, a newspaper over his face. We can tell by the surroundings and the background noise that this is a different time. The occasional honking of an old time auto horn distant in the background lets us know that we have entered a more recent time frame.

Presently, a man in uniform enters the scene showing the recent entry from the jacket down, as he slowly walks toward Rags. The policeman then gently taps the bench that Rags is sleeping on with his nightstick and says in a kind and cheerful voice.

Policeman: O.k. Rags, you had better be getting up now. All your friends are here and they'll be wanting their breakfast.

With this Rags slowly and without alarm sits up and stretches. While he is stretching he speaks.

Rags: I must have fallen asleep. Trying to avoid work all day can sure tire a man out. *(looking down now at the usual assortment of pigeons and squirrels).* And what do you guys want...I know...I know...

Reaching into his pocket Rags comes up with a handful of corn and seeds. Now sitting up and completely awake he sits upon the park bench leaned over. His feet apart and his elbows on his knees he spreads the seeds upon the ground and watches as the animals pick away at the offering. By this time the noise is increasing as the avenue in front of the park, and the park itself becomes busy with people as they start their day going to their jobs, which for most of them will be at the local brake shoe factory. And for as many as pass by, Rags greets with both a tip of the hat and a pleasant smile. With a sigh of contentment he looks at the factory which can be seen from the park but which is at the other end of town. Two workers walk by. It is they who initiate todays greeting.

First Worker: 'Morning Rags.

Rags acknowledges with a tip of his hat and a smile.

Second Worker: How does he do it? He hangs around all day, never works, yet never seems to want for anything. And he has that same contented grin on his face every single morning.

With this greeting Rags raises himself from the bench and stretches. Then he starts toward the street which is now busy with the mixed traffic of horses, and cars, trolleys and the like. He nears the edge of the road when suddenly he sees a small dog in imminent danger and about to be destroyed by an oncoming runaway horse and wagon. The dog is very young and so frightened that he cowers and is frozen in the horse's path. Acting out of instinct alone Rags bolts out into the road. Diving, he grabs the small dog as he rolls himself and the animal out of the path of the oncoming runaway all in one expert motion. Completely covered in dust he lays in the gutter of the road. He looks down only to see the puppy sitting safely on his (Rags), stomach. Picking himself up he emerges out of the dirt and dust with the puppy intact. As he adjusts himself, the puppy gives him a lick on the face. Rags shies back at the puppy's offering. In his burly and crass voice he speaks.

Rags: If I had known you were going to do that I wouldn't have saved you, …you fuzzy little creep.

A little boy comes running toward Rags holding and pulling his mother by the hand, harder and harder, until finally he lets go of her and runs full speed toward Rags and the dog.

Billy: Mister, mister…mister!

As the boy runs up to Rags in this moment of excitement he goes from full speed to no speed instantly.

Rags: I know, I know…This is your dog. Well here, you better take this little mutt and hold onto him. I'm getting too old for this, and exertion is really kind of against my nature.

With this Rags kind of reaches out with the young dog toward Billy who reaches up and takes the puppy. Billy takes the dog and hugs it. The puppy goes crazy licking his face and wagging his tail. Billy, while still under the puppy's attack of affection manages to talk to Rags.

Billy: Thank you mister…Oh mister, thank you.

By now the woman who was holding Billy's hand while he was running has caught up to them. She is a younger widow type, wearing a full lavender dress and matching broad rimmed hat that ties under the chin with a wide band of lace. She is Billy's mom.

Mom: It was very good of you to save Billy's dog. You are a very courageous man. How can we thank you?

Rags: Don't mention it. I enjoy jumping in the dirt and nearly having a heart attack. I try to do it at least once a day. That way if an emergency ever arises I'll be ready for it.

Billy's mom along with a few passersby who have stopped to observe these strange goings on laugh at the remarks and the tension of the scene is ended.

Rags

Mom: Please, be kind enough to join us tonight for dinner, and I will not take no for an answer.

Rags: (with reluctance) Well…err…

But before Rags can get his refusal out, Billy speaks. His voice is pleading but full of excitement.

Billy: …Please…mister.

Mom: In fact I insist. We live on Main Street in the big old grey house on the other side of town. Tonight, five thirty, we'll expect you. *(as she speaks she grasps Billy's hand and is walking away. She turns back and with a reassuring smile.)* Don't forget…five thirty.

Rags, who hasn't even been able to answer, just stands there. His hat tilted on the back of his head and with his hands on his hips he mutters to himself.

Rags: I should have known. There would be one more puppy in puppy heaven if I had.

Now taking his hat off, he brushes the dust off of the front of his trousers.

Rags: Dogs… Women…Dinner…*(sighs, looks up toward the sky, and shakes his head)*. I don't know if I'll be able to fit it into my busy schedule. What day is it anyway?

With this Rags walks away. Down the street he goes to start his daily visits with the local shopkeepers. He will carry with him this day, as he does on every day, the answers to all the problems of the town, the country, the world, and the universe. And as always he will be willing to share them with anyone who will stand still long enough to listen.

Chapter 25
The Barber Shop

Inside the local barber shop John the barber is dozing in his own barber chair. The overhead fan is lazily turning while the old potbelly stove that is used to heat the shop each winter stands idle toward the center rear of the shop.

Suddenly the door abruptly opens and Rags enters as a startled barber John slips from his chair.

Barber John: Must have dozed off there for a minute. Guess it's the effect of the sunlight through the window. Seems to be happening more lately. Boy, to be young again. What do you think Rags?

Rags: Ah!! If you've seen one head of hair, you've seen 'em all.

Barber John: (with a smile as he gets a white towel) Guess so Rags. Rags, what brings you in today, 'taint Saturday?

Rags looking a little embarrassed and groping for some answer other than the truth, that might be half believable, stammers.

Rags: Well…err…see…I got a …Well, tonight I have to go somewhere and…err Saturday I think I will be a little busy so…err…I just thought I'd come early this week. Can't pass by a good haircut and shave at least once a week you know.

Rags climbs into the chair as Barber John drapes him with the towel. He starts to give Rags a haircut.

Barber John: What's her name?

Rags: There ain't no her.

Barber John: O.k., whatever you say.

Barber John continues to cut his hair. Then he tilts the barber chair back and begins to lather up the face of Rags.

Barber John: …hairs startin' to look a little thin…

Rags: You know, John, today's just not going to be my day. I can tell… really I can.

Barber John starts to strap the razor on the long leather strap that is hanging on the side of the chair. The slapping of the razor against the leather strap as he sharpens it seems to add some credence to what Rags has just said. Then John starts to shave off the lather. He stands back for a moment.

Barber John: Aw…It's going to be a great day. *(as he finishes shaving Rags).* What could go wrong around here?

Barber John walks over to Rags with a hot towel and puts the towel in a coil over the face of Rags. At that very moment Billy bursts into the shop.

Billy: Hi, Barber John!

Rags: (muffled from under the hot towel) Oh my God, he's back.

Billy: Barber John, I just came by to get the stove ready for the winter. You still want me to tend to 'er like last winter don't you Barber John?

Barber John: Sure do, Billy. Hate having to get up early on those cold days and get that old stove going. You get it started in the morning and then tend it on your way home from school each day. I'll bank the fire at night before I leave for home myself. You've got the job for as long as you want it.

Billy: Thank you, Barber John.

Billy then rushes around cleaning out the old stove with a small black shovel. He works just as fast as he can. Then he turns and runs out of the shop only to return almost instantly.

Billy: Barber John, did you hear about my dog? He got saved today.

As Billy darts out of the shop for the second time John removes the towel from Rags' face.

Rags: John, who is that? Is that your kid?

Barber John: (laughing) No Rags, this old man…ha…I wish. No that's Billy. Lives at the end of town in that big old grey house. You know who his father was? Do you remember that young guy that used to hang out in the candy store? Well, I don't know if you remember but he went off into the army soon after his wedding. Got killed. Billy never really knew his father. Now it's just him and his mom. He's really a great little kid, tries so hard to be a man at home. Shines shoes here in the shop from time to time when he's not in school. And he and that little mutt of his …boy if anything ever happened to that dog I think he'd die. Someone saved his dog today?…Didn't just save a dog, saved a boy.

Rags is now out of the chair and reaching into his pocket for money to pay the barber for his haircut and shave. After hearing what the barber has said his attitude has changed somewhat. He is more sober, and in a more sober voice.

Rags: Thanks, John.

Rags now leaves the shop and as he does he wanders down the road and sees Billy running after the local ice wagon with his puppy in hot pursuit. Billy running, catches up to the slow moving wagon. There is a wooden bucket filled with ice chips and pieces near the back of the ice wagon. He half climbs aboard and is successful in getting a loose piece of ice for himself and another smaller piece which he throws back to his puppy. The driver of the wagon pretends to be unaware. An understanding smile softens the face of Rags. Billy and his dog are content to enjoy the cool ice they have just pilfered. And although the end does not justify the means nevertheless the end, in this case, seems rather harmless. Rags smiles. He has just seen a young boy catch his first fish; see his first planted seed sprout; steal his first piece of summer ice.

Just then the twelve o'clock whistle from the brake shoe factory cuts through the afternoon noise. Rags turns toward the factory. His hat is tilted on the back of his head. He glances upward at the big sign on the factory. At this point through his eyes we see what he sees, "The J.J. Jenkins Train and Brake Shoe Factory." A memory crosses his mind. He quietly smiles to himself.

Chapter 26
The J.J. Jenkins Train and Brake Shoe Factory

We go back in time in our story and pass beyond the eyes of the person looking up at the sign and there with his hands on his hips and with a look of pride on his face stands our stoic bearded friend, Joshua, sweat rolling down his face, his hat tilted on the back of his head. Joshua has just finished putting up the sign for the "J.J. Jenkins Train and Brake Shoe Factory." He retrieves a large red polka dot handkerchief from out of his pocket and wipes his face. Then he puts it back into his pocket. As he does so he turns and speaks.

Joshua: What do you think, Sara?

Sara: It's beautiful, Joshua. I'm so proud of you. You must feel so good inside.

Joshua: Sara, do you remember when we came to this town? Just me, you, and a wagon full of earthlies. Remember how Eddie took us to see Mr. Brown, rest his soul, and how we lived in the little cottage. He was a good man, true to his word. Now there are three of us and we have so much to be thankful for. We have so much more now, but those were beautiful days. Sometimes I miss them. Honest.

Sara: Me too. But you know, Joshua, we've already done yesterday and tomorrow still needs doing.

Joshua walks over to Sara. They are a little older now. He walks over to her and hugs her. Then they start to walk away. As they walk together we can hear Joshua speaking to Sara.

Joshua: Sara, can I ask you something?

Sara: Why not Josh. *(turning her head toward him)*

Joshua: Why did you give my only son Isaac, the nickname Rags?

Sara: (laughing) Well, Joshua, it's a good Christian name.

Joshua: Come on now Sara, the truth. I'm too old to be playing games and every time I ask I get a different answer. Once and for all Sara, say it just as it is.

Sara: Josh, you know…people are just like rags; different shapes, different sizes, different colors and made of different material. But somehow God takes all these different remnants and sews them together, and behold by his hand the most beautiful quilt ever is made. All the colors and shapes and sizes are drawn together and they each have a place and together they make the quilt. He has sewn a beautiful work of art. I guess I just wanted him to know that the material we made was for him to use according to his good will and pleasure. I just don't know what could be more beautiful than that. I think Rags is a beautiful name.

Joshua pauses for a moment and looks at Sara.

Joshua: Only you Sara…only you. Beyond any shadow of a doubt, an angel right here on earth.

Sara looks up at Joshua with a coy and smiling look.

Sara: And who knows Joshua J. Jenkins hard as it may be to imagine but one day our little Rags might have a few patches of his own.

Joshua: Sara…*(sigh)*…Sara, I'm glad I stole you away when I did. I stole you right out of Heaven.

Joshua then helps Sara up onto the wagon which is waiting nearby. After helping her up he walks around to the back of the wagon where a cute little tot dressed in coveralls and a straw hat is sitting with one arm around a big collie type dog. It is Isaac. Joshua moves quietly to the little guy, snatches him up in a very playful manner, grabs him under the arms, and throws him into the air catching him and tickling him. The boy laughs more and more as his dad plays with him. The dog wagging his tail barks each time the boy is lifted into the air, showing his concern for his young companion.

Joshua: (to the lad) Are you ready to go home and get some supper old man.

Isaac: (shyly laughing) Yes, daddy.

Playfully Joshua roughens the hair on the collies head as he pets him. Then moving to the driver's seat he turns to them and says.

Joshua: Hang on! We're on our way to the "good room" and mamas good cooking.

The wagon pulls away with everyone smiling, Sara next to Joshua on the front seat and the little boy still in the back of the wagon sitting with his arm once more around his friend the collie. Soon the wagon pulls up to their almost frontier looking home. The boy bounces off of the back of the wagon at the same time as the dog. They race to the door and enter the house. Josh and Sara follow. Once inside the house Josh sits in his rocking chair smoking his pipe, and little Isaac sits on the floor hugging and playing with his dog. Mama has just finished putting the last of the dishes of food on the table.

Sara: I would like to have all of my men come to the table now before I decide to eat all of this good food myself.

Josh puts down his pipe and rises. The little guy has already jumped up onto his chair at the table. Joshua takes his place at the head of the table. The dog is right next to the boy wagging his tail while sitting down and looking up directly at the boy. The dog gives a soft bark.

Isaac: Shhhh…*(in a whisper to the dog)* We have to say grace first.

After this they all sit quietly and automatically wait. It is time for grace. They focus on the bread at the table.

Joshua: Most holy and gracious Father in Heaven. We thank you for sharing this abundance with us that it might strengthen us. And that in that strength we find always the strength to stand fast…..

Chapter 27
The Invitation. Rags Tells His Family History

Mom: ....on our believing. We thank you for this opportunity to come together and to share with each other all that you have made available through your son our Lord and Savior the risen Christ Jesus...Amen.

We are back in the present with Rags, Billy and his mom saying grace before dinner. Rags has been invited to dinner. We see Rags, Billy and his mom seated at the table which is all set, ready to eat.

Mom: Billy, please pass the potatoes to Mr......?

Rags: Rags ma'am. People just call me Rags, ma'am.

Mom: ...To Mr. Rags.

Billy: (as he passes the potatoes, with the pride of a young boy passing food, or better yet serving his hero, he cannot restrain himself as he Blurts Out) WHAT A GREAT NAME!!

Mom: (in a slightly reprimanding tone) Billy.......

Billy: Yes, ma'am.

Rags: (smiling) Thank you, Billy. *(as he receives the potatoes)*

Mom: It was really a brave thing you did today. Billy, say your piece now.

Rags

Billy rises off of his chair and goes over to his puppy. Picking up the pup and holding it in his arms he walks over and stands in front of Rags. Rags lowers his fork.

Billy: Rags,…Boxcar and I would like to thank you for what you did today. You saved the one person in the world that is my best'ist friend. We love you and we thank you.

Without speaking Rags is taken back. He opens his arms and hugs the both of them. Then Rags clears his throat as Billy returns to his place at the table.

Rags: (clearing his throat) Hmmm…hmm…

As dinner continues the conversation that was initially trying becomes easier and the relationship between Billy and Rags starts to warm up naturally. Rags addresses Billy.

Rags: Hey young fella. I understand that you are quite a worker. Why I hear tell that you give the best shoe shine in all of Massachusetts and that you are great at stoking a stove. *(Billy beams at the compliment)* Tell you what. I know a few people and if you ever want some extra work after school let me know. *(Billy is ecstatic)*

Billy: (excited) I work for Barber John sometimes after school. *(proud)* And in the winter, in the mornings, I tend the stove.

Rags: That's great. Then I can tell my friend that you have experience. He'll like that.

Mom: I don't know what to say. Heaven knows we can use the money. Billy is quite a help to me. He's my big man now.

Billy: Thank you, Rags.

Rags: Life can get a little trying at times. *(changes the subject)* You know, here I am all this time and I don't know your name.

Mom: Martha.

Rags: Martha, you have a very nice home and a very nice family. And best of all now I can call you Martha, and not Billy's mom, from now on.

Mom: Thank you, Rags. And yes, sometimes it's trying. We do miss Billy's dad but we've learned to manage. The Lord watches over us. We've learned to rely on him and each other. We're blessed to have enough to share. More coffee?

Rags: Sure, it's great. An old loner like me don't get treated to this kind of meal and fine service very often. You gonna spoil me. Ya know, you don't miss what you don't know.

Mom: Why you come by any time, Rags. We both like having you here very much.

Rags: Ma'am I didn't mean…*(cut off by Martha)*

Mom: Fiddle sticks, we'd love to have you.

Rags just nods his head in appreciation.

Mom: Billy, why don't you take Mr. Rags into the big room while I clean up.

Rags: Can I help you clean the table at least?

Mom: Get…Get…*(gesturing for them to go)*

Billy and Rags go off into the living room. Rags sits in a big overstuffed chair as Billy settles himself on the floor in front and to the side of Rags. His little dog comes over also, very content after having had a very good dinner, and settles next to Billy. Billy looks up at Rags in a very puzzled manner. There is something Billy wants to know. Not wanting to hurt Rags' feelings he speaks gently in a soft questioning voice.

Billy: Rags? Why are you a loner? *(obviously picking up from the dinner conversation)*

Rags: I guess because I don't have any real family.

Rags

Billy: Me either.

Rags: What do you mean? You have Boxcar and your mom. She's a great lady.

Billy: Yeah, but you know what I mean. Other kids have grandfathers and fathers. Rags, do you have a grandfather or a father?

Rags: A long time ago, Billy…See my pop went to Heaven before I was really old enough to know him. But I do remember my grandfather.

Billy: What's a grandfather like?

Rags: Well, they're usually kind of old. And kids love 'em.

Billy: Like you?

Rags: (with a smile) Like me.

Billy: Rags, what was your grandfather like?

Rags pauses. For a moment he just sits back in his chair with his eyes closed. He sighs as he opens his eyes. As he does he looks upward, but after a moment glances down at the boy. He fixes himself in the chair and folds his hands in front of him and then with a deep sincerity begins.

Rags: His name was Joshua…Joshua J. Jenkins. He was quite a guy, Billy. Actually he was originally from a place not far from here, Hancock. He used to tell me about that place. He was a great man, a good looking man, stern and strong and very, very wise. The people that he lived with in the village that he came from were really quite religious and quite industrious. They were called "Shakers", yep, "Shakers". They were quite a group I'll tell you. Peace loving, good people. You know the chairs that we sat on at dinner were first made in that design by them. Perfection and simplicity, I can't begin to tell you how often I heard Grandpa Joshua say that over and over to me. Perfection and simplicity: simplicity and perfection. Grandpa liked sayings like that. He would often say things like, "Hands to work and hearts to God". He was a good teacher by example. Most times he never had to say anything. All you ever really had to do to learn anything from old Grandpop Joshua was to watch. He was a marvel. Not so much with what he said but with what he did. The packages of seeds that you buy down at the hardware store for growing vegetables and flowers, well his people were the very first to put those seeds in those little packages and sell them. They thought up and invented device after device to make life better, and work easier. For example, they invented the circular saw. Did you ever see that big circular saw down at the saw mill? Well, they made that. Before, men had to cut all those boards by hand. And I bet you never gave a second thought about where the clothespin came from that your mom uses to hang out the wash. Well old J.J., that's what people liked to call him, J.J. Well, Josh and his Shaker friends invented them and lots more.

Billy: Grandfathers do all those things.

Rags: Well, maybe not all grandfathers. But Shaker grandfathers didn't seem to know any better. They just kept inventing things. The flat broom that mom uses. The mechanical washing machine... But anyway the people at the village had one shortcoming. They didn't like to make little people from big people, and end up with beautiful people like you. This was part of their religious belief. But that just wasn't Grandpa Joshua's way. See grandpa was in love with Sara, a beautiful girl that he loved ever since he was a little boy. That was my grandma, Billy. She and Josh grew up together. See at the village the men and women were together, but separate. Even in church they would sit on opposite sides of the room to worship. Well, old Grandpa Joshua loved Sara, so one day *(Rags leans forward and smiles as he speaks)* while Sunday service was going on Sara sneaks out the back door of the congregation and meets

Rags

ole Josh in the barn out behind the house where he had loaded all their earthly possessions onto the back of the wagon, and they run off together to make a life for themselves. I remember how he told me they traveled day and night until they reached this very town. *(Rags once again leans back into his chair).* He went to work for the railroad for a while. Yep, for Mr. Beaumont Brown himself. Mr. Beaumont was familiar with the mechanical abilities and the creative ability of the Shaker men. And he was having some trouble with the braking system on his trains. So he put old J.J. to work on it. Well, before you could say Boxcar, J.J. was busy building a better and safer system. Well the railroad chief liked it, and so grandpa and Mr. Brown started manufacturing their type of brakes for the railroads. Then when Mr. Brown passed on he left the company to J.J.... Can you keep a secret?

Billy: Yes...Yes.

Rags: Cross your heart and hope your nose grows on backwards if you tell?

Billy: (crossing his heart) Cross my heart.

Rags: I'm going to trust you with a secret that I've never told anyone. It was my grandfather Joshua that started the very same brake shoe factory that's in this town.

Billy: Wow!

Rags: Well, Grandpa Josh and Sara had a good life here Billy. And they did have a little boy. That was my father. His name was Isaac. Grandpa used to tell me all about him every chance he'd get. Kind of just like I'm telling you. He wanted so much for me to be as proud of him as he was.

Billy: You mean you didn't know your father either?

Rags: That's right, Billy. All I ever knew about my father was what J.J. told me. He grew up helping and running the factory with grandpa. Those are treasured memories. He loved my dad so much. Sara, my grandma, used to call my father Rags just like me. Actually that's how I got the name.

(The scenes that follow are the story of Rags' family history. They take place in the past, and alternate with his narration, which is in the present.)

The scene is a flashback to a screen door of a back porch. Sara is holding the door open and waiting as Isaac, the father of our Rags, comes down the stairs fixing his tie as he hurries toward the door. He is a young adult.

Sara: Isaac, don't forget your lunch pail.

As Isaac goes through the door that Sara is holding open she hands him his lunch pail. Joshua is already outside. Isaac half running looks back and waves goodbye while catching up to Joshua. They both head off toward the factory walking through the same park that opened the scene with Rags sleeping on the bench. But of course the setting now is of a much earlier time.

Narration Rags: (continues) Dad met my mom one time when they went into Boston on a business trip.

As they walk, father and son, Joshua and Isaac talk.

Joshua: You know I have to go to Boston to finish some business on Thursday. I want you to come with me.

Isaac: Really, great...but why?

Joshua: It's time that you got involved with every aspect of the business. You know I'm not going to be here forever. And if I don't show you where all the stones are, how can I teach you to walk on water?

Isaac: Thursday...great.

As the men enter the factory various men greet them... hello, morning, etc. Each man, Joshua and Isaac, goes into a separate office, each with a glass door and a name on it. Joshua goes into the president's office while Isaac goes into the shop manager's office. The factory is a busy place as the work day starts up. Inside the factory we can see the grinding machines, chains, heavy tools and the like. There is a locomotive right inside the factory on the tracks that pass right through the factory. Men have started their work on the braking system of the train using heavy wrenches and working together on the heavier parts.

In his office Joshua is hanging up his jacket on the coat tree preparing to get into his work day.

Joshua: Emma, get all of the correspondence concerning the signing of the contracts with Mr. Beal of Boston. I'll be going up there on Thursday… Taking Isaac with me, Emma. *(Emma smiles as she gets his things together)*

The next scene is from inside of a railroad car. Both Isaac and Joshua are seated quietly, as Isaac, seated in the window seat, stares out at the marvelous scenery as the train rolls on.

Porter: Boston! All out for Boston and all points east…Next stop Paris France…

Isaac excitedly grasps his hat and jacket in contrast to Joshua who is relaxed as one who has done this many times. Joshua rises out of his seat and stretches in the aisle before starting to exit. Isaac smiles.

Isaac: Let's go.

There are many people who are waiting outside the train for the passengers to depart. One person stands out from the rest. He is very well dressed and legal looking. This is the person who is obviously waiting for Joshua. His demeanor is relaxed, as they have obviously done this many times before. This well dressed gentleman is standing with his niece, a lovely young lady who just happens to be the same age as Isaac. The two men see each other and walk toward each other smiling and shaking hands as they meet. Then the young people are introduced. Isaac falls in love instantly. Lightning has struck…and Isaac has had it.

Joshua: Mr. Beal, I'd like to have you meet my son, Isaac.

Mr. Beal: Pleased to meet you, Isaac. I've heard so much about you. It's my pleasure. *(they exchange handshakes)*

Mr. Beal: This is my lovely niece, Anna. Anna,…Joshua…Isaac. *(again they exchange courtesies)*

Mr. Beal: Come, my coach is waiting.

The coach and coachman await them. They get in and then the coach makes its way through the quaint old streets of Boston. The feel of the cobblestone street can be felt and heard beneath the wheels of the coach which after a short scenic ride pulls up in front of a brownstone home in a very nice area of town. It is obvious by the surroundings that this is a well to do neighborhood. The coach pulls up to the curb and stops. Without hesitation the coachman hustles down to open the doors. They exit the coach and approach the neat brownstone steps dressed with wrought iron rails and ivy. Flowers are in the window boxes beneath the beautiful arched windows. The rich mahogany door is accented by the glitter of the fine and massive brass knocker that adorns it. The door opens as they approach even before anyone has occasion to knock. Sophia, a black maid has opened the door. They enter the house and as they do Sophia greets them taking their hats and coats as they enter.

Mr. Beal: Well now, how about something cool to drink. It's rather warm out there today. Sophia, please get Mr. Jenkins and his son here, something cool to drink.

Sophia: (smiling) Certainly.

Mr. Beal: It really did warm up, didn't it. Joshua…Isaac, if you want to wash up before lunch, feel free, please…use the washroom at the end of the hall. Anna, show our guests into the living room.

At this point Joshua goes to the washroom and Anna takes Isaac by the arm and escorts him into the parlor. Her uncle follows. Isaac's face turns red. As she seats him next to her, he fumbles trying to act at ease by making conversation. At this point Isaac has lost it for a bit. He says things that are almost correct but really quite dumb. However the situation is fully understood by Anna and more than tolerated. Her class shows through as she covers for Isaac effortlessly.

Isaac: This room…*(he pulls at his collar)*…is really quite refreshing…*(his tone is quiet and shy)*

Mr. Beal turns his head pretending not to have heard. Anna understands what is happening making it all o.k. and puts Isaac at ease.

Anna: How was your trip to Boston?

Isaac: Oh, fine…really, fine…no problem.

Anna: Uncle tells me that you live in Springfield, or is it Pittsfield?

Isaac: Springfield. *(Isaac feels better now that he has had an opportunity to add input in terms of a correction to the conversation. He does not realize that Anna did this with exactly this purpose in mind.)*

Anna: Oh…It must be nice there.

Isaac: Very.

With this Joshua has returned to the room.

Mr. Beal: (as he rises up out of his chair) How are you

doing? *(he puts his arm around Joshua).* Anna, Isaac...Josh and I are going into the den to talk over old times. *(thus leaving the two alone to get better acquainted)*

Anna: Isaac, would you like to sit out on the back porch? Come, it's really nice out there. It's all screened in and it overlooks the garden. The flowers are beautiful this year, especially the roses.

Anna and Isaac get up and go to the porch behind the house. There they sit in the cool of its shade with their cool drinks overlooking the beauty of the floral array of the garden. They look at the garden. There is no dialogue. After the quietness and beauty of the scene takes over they then look at each other. Now eye to eye they come closer, and Isaac and Anna kiss. Afterwards Isaac is a little flustered. He is worried that he may have in some way offended Anna.

Isaac: I'm sorry...if I...

But again, she kisses him just as if they had been lovers forever. Anna is in love.

As they embrace, their background is the beautiful garden with all of its flowers and greenery. Their embrace is stationary as they are superimposed on the background which continually changes from one beautiful part of the garden to another.

Narration Rags: (continues) Mom and Dad immediately fell in love, and soon after they were married.

The next scene is the garden again. Little has changed within the garden itself except that now there is a wedding and wedding reception going on there. It is one year later and the wedding is that of Isaac and Anna. They are at the end of the aisle made by the wooden straight back chairs on the lawn. The minister has just pronounced them man and wife and the kiss which started in the previous scene ends. They turn, Anna in her beautiful white wedding gown and Isaac in his formal coat and tails. As they walk back down the aisle, away from the minister, the people in the chairs in random order rise to congratulate them. Everyone is very, very happy. People are hugging and congratulating them. Everyone is dressed up. It is a beautiful wedding.

There is a table to the side where a butler tends to the champagne glasses which are upon it. Sophia moves through the small but crowded garden among the guests with a tray of cookies and bits of food.

Mr. Beal moves to the table where the glasses of champagne are. Taking a glass and raising it he shouts out over the mumble and laughter of his guests.

Mr. Beal: To the new Mr. and Mrs. Jenkins. May your lives be ever blessed with love and happiness.

Everyone cheers and toasts the two, and at that very moment the string ensemble with flute and French horns begins playing. Waltzes and perfume fill the air of the garden this day. It is the wedding day of Isaac and Anna.

Mr. Beal: (talking to Joshua) Did you ever think it would come to this?

Joshua: And I thought I was taking him on a business trip. Kids!... You send them to the store for one thing and they always come home with something else.

Both Joshua and Mr. Beal enjoy a laugh. It is a happy time.

Mr. Beal: They should have a wonderful time at the cottage. I had Sophia and Turrel go out there earlier this week to prepare it for them. There's everything they will need there.

Joshua: I doubt that they'll even notice. It should be beautiful by the ocean this week.

Mr. Beal: Yes, the weather is supposed to be good. Although you're right, I doubt they'll even notice.

Mr. Beal and Joshua part and Joshua makes his way over to Sara as Mr. Beal mingles with the guests.

Sara: Have you ever seen anyone as much in love as those two?

Joshua: Yes. Once I knew a boy and a girl. The boy stole this girl away in the back of his wagon.

Sara: She must have been very willing to let herself be stolen away like that.

Joshua: I suppose. But then as I recall the boy was quite good looking…she probably couldn't help herself.

Sara: (laughs) Do you think there will be any mice on their honeymoon?

They both laugh just as they did when they were younger. As they do, the sound of their laughter gives way to the cry of seagulls. In the sky we see a gentle flying gull as it soars, then lands on the beautiful rolling waves of the ocean. The beach is in view and we see Isaac and Anna running and enjoying themselves in the ruffle of the last bit of waves as they reach out and then disappear in the sand. Now hand in hand they come to a stop, half out of breath, and face each other. For the moment they just look at each other without speaking. Then Isaac softly speaks.

Isaac: I wish it would never end.

Anna runs her hand up to Isaac's shoulder and as she approaches his lips with hers she half whispers to him.

Anna: It never will…I promise. *(they kiss)*

After they break they continue to walk. After a short time

they come upon a man surf casting. They stop and watch him for a moment. Then they politely ask him how he is doing.

Isaac: (to the fisherman) How's it going? They biting?

Fisherman: Just the flies… keep stealin' my bait…On vacation?

Isaac: Kind of…

Fisherman: Be here long?

Isaac: This is our last night. Tomorrow it's back to work. Hate to go.

Fisherman: I know what you mean. The fish are on vacation also. Wonder if they'll ever come back.

Isaac: Well, good luck. Hope you catch a big one.

They wave, as Isaac and Anna walk away picking up shells as they go.

Isaac: Well, tomorrow it's back home for us. Anna you are going to love it in Springfield. It will be great living with Joshua and Sara.

Anna: I'm sure it will be Isaac. Do you think that one day we will have a place of our own?

Isaac: I'm sure we will.

As he is speaking they have reached the steps of the seaside cottage. Isaac turns to Anna and continues speaking.

Isaac: I was waiting. I mean I guess that makes it official.

Anna: What do you mean?

Isaac: I mean every married man must be asked that question before his marriage is considered official…Boy, am I relieved.

Anna: Isaac you are impossible…for anyone but me that is.

Rags

She takes him by the hand and leads him inside the cottage.

Narrator Rags: (continues) Then Isaac and Anna moved into the old house with Grandpa Josh and Sara.

We now move to Joshua's home. We are in the kitchen. The four; Joshua, Sara, Isaac, and Anna are happily moving about the kitchen of the old house. It is evident that Isaac and Anna are attempting to settle down and into their new lives as newlyweds. Anna is wearing an apron. It is early in the morning and unlike other mornings Isaac is leaving for the factory before Joshua. As he exits the screen door, Anna hands him his lunch pail. He kisses his wife on the cheek and they wave goodbye as he goes off to work. As is the usual case we follow him rapidly through the park and into the factory. In his usual hurried way he enters into his office ready to take on the challenges of the day. Little does he realize that the challenges of this particular day will end in complete disaster and will cost him his life. Precious as it was when it started, this day will be short for Isaac and will live in the memory of those who remain and will still love him.

Isaac leaves his office and enters into the factory proper to go about this day's business. A man is working with some heavy object which is being lifted by a chain attached to an old wooden block and tackle. As he guides the part toward the train, the frame holding and supporting the entire mass gives way crushing the poor fellow. As he goes down he inadvertently kicks over a can of flammable fluid which ignites as sparks from a nearby worker hit the fluid. Suddenly there is an explosion as more of the fluids ignite and the wooden structure, dry and old, starts to burn rapidly. Someone is yelling 'FIRE! FIRE!' as panic ensues. Isaac reacting rushes over in a futile effort to control the rapidly raging fire. His efforts are useless and he is forced to retreat because of the intense heat of the fire.

Rags

Several men have been trying to help Isaac control the flames but realize the hopelessness of the situation and retreat also in the heat of the flames. By now the fire is raging and completely out of control. As they retreat one workman slips and a huge timber falls onto him. He screams, and as he does, Isaac tries desperately to save him. He works in the face of extreme heat, his face charred and his hair partially burnt. Several men return to try and help Isaac free the unfortunate worker. They seem even in the face of such a bad situation to be making some headway as the beam seems now to be moving as they strain to lift it and free the injured soul. Suddenly, as unexpected as you can imagine, just at the point of them achieving freedom, the entire wood frame gives way and Isaac as well as several of the workers who tried to help him are engulfed by the fiery jaws of death . They are literally swallowed up in the inferno. There is no question in anyone's mind at this moment that they are gone.

Narration Rags: (This narration by Rags has been going on throughout the fire scene) Seems one day dad had to go to work early. It started out as just another regular day, nothing special. Dad had just come back from his honeymoon with mom. Seems he had to go to work early that day. Me, well I was just a bump in my mother's apron at the time but no one knew it yet. Not even mom. Well, Billy, tragedy came to Springfield that day. I don't know why tragedy happens, sometimes it just happens. There was a terrible accident at the plant that day. A real bad accident. Seems some fluid used for oiling and cleaning parts exploded when supports gave out. They ignited, fire broke out and my father died trying to save some of the workers who were injured. It was terrible. Mom couldn't stay around because she couldn't bear to be around without dad so she moved back to Boston to live. Seemed grandpa and grandma had lost everything; their only son who they loved so very, very much and also the factory and business that it took Joshua so long to build. It was a bad time.

(The scene continues)

Sadness reeks over the home of Joshua and Sara as Sara quietly moves about the kitchen meaninglessly putting things away and Joshua sits just staring from the big old chair. From where Joshua is sitting we see Sara go out the front door. We hear the screen door lightly bang shut as the inner door remains open allowing us to watch. We can see her make her way to the mail box in front of their home. She removes the letters from the box and stands for a moment as she reads the letter heads seeing what came today. Suddenly she comes upon one letter and stops. She returns to the house with much more energy than when she left. As she enters back through the open door she is already opening the letter that has caught her attention. She tears at the envelope in a rushed but gentle manner. As she does this she is making her way toward Joshua. However she stops as she has now fully retrieved the pages from within prior to reaching where Joshua is sitting. She reads. And there in the sad quietness of the J.J. Jenkins home, without a sound the tears begin to roll down the sad but beautiful cheeks of the warm and saintly woman. As the tears continue to fall her lips form into an almost forgotten smile. Now hardly being able to hold back her emotions she grabs her apron and rushes to Joshua's darkened room. Rushing to him, she stops before him. And in her loving way pleads through her tears in a thankful whisper.

Sara: Oh, Joshua.......Anna's pregnant.

Joshua looks up and starts to come to life. He rises and moves to Sara as he anxiously takes the letter. He reads for a moment, and as he does, the tears begin to form and roll down his now leathery face. He turns to Sara, letter still in hand, and wraps both of his arms around her holding and hugging her tighter and tighter. This new life that has begun, is the new beginning of life for Sara and Joshua. For soon there is to be a new son; and a new grandson.

(We at this point revert back to the original narration)

Narration Rags: (continues) The only thing that saved it for them was a letter they received from mom telling them she was carrying me. Old grandpa went to Boston that very same day and convinced mom to move back with them. Grandpa Josh, who was a man of his word, promised mom that day, that he would rebuild the plant and that there would never be anything that she or her new baby would ever want.

(the scene continues)

Joshua is home in the kitchen. He is holding a new born baby in his arms. Sara is at his side. She has just handed the child to him. Sara looks on with joy. The joy of the new life has spread and has now overcome the forgotten sadness of the moment. This new life is received with love. She lovingly reaches over to touch the baby and as she does she whispers.

Sara: …Rags…*(she looks up to Heaven)*…For your beautiful quilt.

The doctor enters from the bedroom to the kitchen with Sophia at his side.

Doctor: She's doing very well. Sophia if you need me for anything…*(Sophia nods)*. Joshua, Sara…Anna is strong. She's doing very good. Let her rest.

The Doctor walks over to the new baby. He looks at Joshua holding the baby, smiles, gives Joshua an acknowledging pat on the arm with his hand, shakes his head in a "yes" and understanding way and leaves.

Narration Rags: (continues) I was born. The doctor said I

was ugly and left me in the arms of my grandfather. He said I was healthy,…but ugly.

Grandpa said that he would never give that old factory a chance to take away his grandson. So he called in Mr. Beal and had some real fancy papers made up so that no one would ever really know who I was with respect to the plant. I guess outside of the family only the doctor and Sophia were the only others who really knew. And Sophia well she was more family than family. That left Doc and he understood the situation and would never say anything. Well, son, Sara started in calling me Rags just like my dad. I'm real proud of that name. Everyone was sure that one day I would also have a patch or two of my own. Well, as fate would have it, it just didn't work out that way. I have no family of my own now.

Billy who is so caught up in the story just blurts out.

Billy: I'll be your family, Rags…I'll be your family… It'll be great…You'll have a family … I need a family, too… Mom will have a family, too …It'll be great…Mom…Mom… *(as he runs to his mother)* …I got a family…and I got a new name, too.

Mom: (looking a bit bewildered) A new name? What new name?

Rags: (as he sinks back into the chair, he says just outside the hearing range of the others in a half whisper) …Oh Shit…

Billy: Patches…Patches…Ma, ain't it great! It's Rags and me, Ma; Patches and Rags.

Rags: (under his breath) At least it could have been Rags and Patches. *(now in a normal volume).* Sorry, ma'am. Guess I got kind of carried away with my story telling. Better be going home now I suspect.

Mom: Rags…please don't rush.

Rags: No ma'am ought to be going now, thank you.

Mom: Rags please, you will come back again? We did so enjoy having you here with us tonight. It was good for Billy,… Patches…and it was good for me also. You have done so much for us, and all in the same day. Thank you.

Martha then gives Rags a friendly kiss on the cheek as they approach the front door.

Rags: (a bit awkward but sincere) Goodnight and thank you.

He turns to leave. Then he turns back in the direction of Billy and pauses…He smiles… looks directly at Billy …

Rags: 'Night Patches.

Billy lights up with a smile. Rags nods and winks as he closes the door.

Chapter 28
The Promise

The night is still except for the sounds of the insects and frogs which softly blend into the velvet cover of the darkness. As he walks, the occasional light from the windows reach out into the night and blend into the quiet canvas of the peaceful evening. Inwardly Rags is very pleased. As he walks, he pauses to listen for a moment to the night sounds. Then he looks up and with a deep sigh he admires the magnificent star lit sky. It is an open sky, clean and brisk, in contrast to the brilliance of the stars that shine out against the deep darkness of the heavens above.

While we focus on the beautiful night sky we hear the voice of a younger adolescent Rags speaking. Now just a boy, standing on the back porch of his home, as he looks up toward the sky, he speaks.

Rags: Mama, did you call?

Anna speaks to the young Rags as she exits the house to where he is. Looking up as she comes to him she answers.

Anna: Yes son.

At this point she is outside and becomes aware of the magnificent evening. Without hesitation she looks up and continues.

Anna: My, what a beautiful night. Why, the stars look bright enough to be the candles on God's birthday cake. They are

Rags

absolutely beautiful……. Rags I think your grandfather would like to talk to you.

Rags: Yes, ma'am.

With this Rags starts toward the lighted door of the kitchen. Anna waits for a moment for Rags to get to where she is. Then as he reaches her she lovingly puts her arm around him and they enter the house together. Rags and Anna pass quickly through the kitchen and into the living room where Joshua and Mr. Beal are both waiting for him.

Rags: Grandpa, you wanted to see me?

Joshua: Yes, son. *(pause)* Rags……..Mr. Beal and I have just finished working out something that is very important to me. Now I know that at first you might not understand all that we are doing but please just trust us for the time being. You see a long time ago we lost your father to a fire at the plant. Well it hurt you, and me, and your mother, and Grandma Sara real bad. So I made a promise to your mother and to Grandma Sara then that I would never take the chance of losing anyone to the factory again.

Mr. Beal: You know Rags, after the fire, well your grandfather started all over again. Actually because of you, and with you and your mom in mind, he developed it into a very prosperous business. Now he's consulted me about how to pass on the prosperity of the business to you and your mom, but also how to get the risk out of owning it. He cares for both of you so much. I'm sure you can appreciate how he feels about what happened. He wants to keep his promise to you, to your mom, and to himself.

Rags: Yes, sir.

Joshua: To do this son, Mr. Beal and I have decided to do the following. First we've set up a company in New York and we have made you the owner of that company. Then we have arranged to have the "Brake Shoe Factory" sold to that New York company. After the sale we will then appear to have no connection with the company that we have just sold... but in fact, you will still own it. But no one will know. We will hire managers to run the plant from the New York office. The plant will always afford a wealth of income for you and your mom but you will not ever have to work there and no one need ever know that you are in fact the owner.

Mr. Beal: You see, Rags, after the terrible tragedy your grandpa just wanted you to enjoy life to its fullest. To live right here in Springfield and take care of your mom. You won't have any financial problems, I've seen to that. Money earned by the plant will continuously be added into a trust account for you and for your mom. You will always have all the money you will ever need and the love and freedom to live life to its fullest.

Joshua: This is something I want to do for you and your mom, Rags. Your father helped make the plant what it is and I really want to do this one thing for him...and for you. It's a promise I made and want to keep. Can you understand?

The flashback ends and we now go back to Rags as he continues his walk back from having dinner with Billy and his mom. As he walks he sighs and speaks softly to himself.

Rags: I understand, grandpa...I understand... *(sigh).* Sure do miss you and mama and Sara though.

Rags walks quietly for a while longer.

Chapter 29
Stretch and Noaccount

Rags continues to walk. He is now approaching the house that we have come to know as the house of Joshua and Sara. Obviously Rags still lives here. As he approaches the steps we hear a noise from behind a large bush nearby.

Behind the bush: …Psst…….Psst…*(in a whisper)*…Rags,…Rags…over here…Psst…over here.

Rags stops and looks toward the bush.

Rags: Who's there? What do you want? Who is that?

He is interrupted by the bush.

Behind the bush: Shhh…Shhh…not so loud.

Rags: Look bush, I don't know for sure who you are, although I think I have a pretty good idea…but there is no one within a mile of us and you're telling me …Shhh…Shhh… I feel like Moses standing here in the middle of the night talking to a bush.

Behind the bush: Shhh…The days have eyes, but the nights have ears.

Rags: Bull donkey…Noaccount, is that you?

Behind the bush: I think so?

Rags: You mean you don't know! That's you! Come out here

dummy. Now what's going on? *(as if saying, "Now what kind of trouble are you in?")*

With this Noaccount comes out from behind the bush and approaches Rags. As he does he starts to speak in a shy way.

Noaccount: Been waiting for you Rags. Where've you been? Been waiting here a long time.

Rags: You've been waiting for me a long time…here… behind the bush.

Noaccount: Yeah. It wasn't too bad actually…*(pause)*…'till that dog came along. I've been blessed.

Rags: Noaccount you will never change. Either you're right and the rest of the world is crazy, or …oh well, just forget it. What are you doing here?

Noaccount: Hey, Rags, you got to help Stretch and me.

Rags: What do you need?

Noaccount: Well, we really don't need nothin'. See Stretch and I, well, we was down by the tracks, you know, where we all hang out and all. Well, we was talking about dying and funerals and such and…

The scene fades to "Hobo Haven" down by the tracks. There in front of a small fire sit two men, Noaccount and Stretch, heating some coffee. They pour some coffee into two cans and then proceed to relax by sitting, one on a rock, and the other on the ground, resting his back against a large old log.

Stretch: Noaccount?

Noaccount: Yeah, Stretch?

Stretch: You know how we are free spirits…

Noaccount: Yeah, you mean like bums?

Stretch: Well not exactly,... but kind of... Do you think if'n we died anyone would come to the funeral?

Noaccount: Absolutely...Let's see, J.P. Morgan... the Pope...We'd have to sell tickets.

Stretch: No, I bet that people would really come.

Noaccount: No way.

Stretch: No, really. I mean we really do know a lot of people actually.

Noaccount: Yeah, only outside of our best friend Rags, no one wants to admit it.

Stretch: That's not true. Why I bet if you died tomorrow that a lot of people would come and pay their respects.

Noaccount: Ha! They'd pee on our grave.

Stretch: See that's your trouble. You have no confidence in the human race.

Noaccount: Oh yeah, I do so. I'm confident they would not come.

Stretch: They would...

Noaccount: Would not...

Stretch: Would...

Noaccount: Would not...

Stretch: (Turning his head as he speaks toward Noaccount, so as to try and get the last word in.) Would so...

Noaccount: No way.

Stretch: Want to bet?

Noaccount: Yes, I'd love to ...but win or lose we would still be in the same place because neither of us has any money.

Stretch: Don't matter, it's the principle of the thing.

Noaccount: Tell you what…I got an idea. Tomorrow I'll go down to the paper and put a notice in it that you died. No one will suspect. I mean we do work at the funeral home part time raking leaves and painting and such. Don't Mr. Dodds down there at the parlor send me over to the paper with notices all the time anyway?

Stretch: Yeah, but he goes away on vacation tomorrow. He told me to come and pick up the keys because he'll be away for 'bout two weeks. Wants us to look after the place while he's gone.

Stretch and Noaccount: (together) **GREAT!**

Noaccount: (laughing) Tomorrow I'm going down to the paper and I'm putting a notice in the obituary that old Stretch has died and that the wake will be held the following day.

Stretch: Wait a minute. Why do I have to die? I mean …I'm so young.

Noaccount: Because you'll be able to do it better than me. You've had more practice. *(laughs)* Hee…Hee… And old Mr. Dodds will be away. We'll see if anyone comes out to see you or not.

Stretch: Too bad we can't make some money out of dying.

Noaccount: Probably can. But since you can't take it with you, just leave it to me.

Stretch: What do you mean we probably can?

Noaccount: Well you know how the guys at the saloon are, they'll bet on anything. Why don't we make book on it. We can give odds on the number of people that show up, then even though they know about it and come, whoever else shows up will change the odds.

Stretch: Noaccount, I can't figure you out sometimes. You swing back and forth from genius to idiot, and idiot to genius.

Tomorrow will be a busy day… can't wait. There will be a lot of people at my funeral. Better bring up the extra chairs from the basement.

Noaccount: Won't need to …

Stretch: Will so…

Noaccount: Won't…

Stretch: Will…

Noaccount: Nope…

Stretch: Yes.

The next scene is that of Stretch and Noaccount raking leaves and trimming the bushes at the funeral home. They are outside working when the door opens and Mr. Dodds exits. He has a suitcase in his hand. As he walks down the sidewalk leading to the road, both Stretch and Noaccount stop working and Mr. Dodds comes over to them.

Mr. Dodds: Now boys I'm going to be away for just two weeks. Here are the keys. Just check around and make sure everything stays quiet and peaceful around here. I don't suspect anyone will be dying on you.

Stretch and Noaccount just look at each other.

Stretch: No need to worry… *(as he takes the keys from Mr. Dodds).* If anything comes in we'll put it on ice for you.

Mr. Dodds: 'Bye boys. I'm just dying to get going.

Stretch and Noaccount look at each other.

Noaccount: You have a good time Mr. Dodds.

With that Mr. Dodds again starts to walk away toward the hearse that is parked at the curb. Waving and throwing his scarf around his neck he enters the hearse and drives off. Stretch and Noaccount look at each other again. Then they look at the

Rags

hearse as it drives out of sight. When it is gone, simultaneously they throw their rakes in the air and, while speaking at almost the same time, dart off in different directions, while yelling to each other.

Noaccount: I'm going to the paper.

Stretch: See you at the saloon. Come there, after.

Noaccount: O.k.

It is the next evening and the funeral home is lit up. The place is, for the lack of a better expression, alive with light and spirit. It is almost festive. People are milling around on the outer steps and we can hear the chatter of those already inside. There are girls from the saloon and some of Noaccount and Stretches gang. Rags is sitting in a chair smoking a big cigar taking it all in. The minister arrives as well as a contingent of women that seem to make it to every funeral no matter who dies. Rags leans over and whispers to Shorty, a friend and member of the click.

Rags: Well, here they come. *(referring to the ladies).* I think they must just keep count or something. I don't think you can die unless you first invite them to the funeral.

Shorty: There goes the ladies auxiliary.

The group of ladies moves toward the front of the room. They gather about the coffin, some with hands over their mouth, some drying prefabricated tears with their hankies. There in the box is Stretch. Everyone is paying their respects, praying, talking and such. High voices from the ladies group can be heard saying…

Voice from the group: My, doesn't he look good. Why he looks just as he did when he was alive. Yes, doesn't he? How peaceful he looks.

Shorty: Oh...Oh...Rags...There goes the widow Jones up to the box.

The widow Jones prim and proper walks out from the group of ladies toward the box. Some of the saloon girls mimic her in the rear of the room giggling as they do it. She walks up to the coffin and is saying her prayers and as she does she gets real close to the body while praying. At this point while she is engrossed in her act old Stretch pops up right into a sitting position. Well the widow Jones just faints straight away right there in front of the coffin. Stretch pops completely out of the box, goes straight for the envelopes and offerings that were left, and invites everyone to the saloon for free drinks.

Stretch: I won! I won! Everybody to the saloon, the drinks are on me. *(as he waves the money and envelopes).*

The minister has fallen to his knees.

Minister: It's a miracle, a miracle!

Rags shakes his head as he rises. He blows some smoke from the cigar out in front of himself and then joins Shorty and the rest as they go out of the house towards the saloon. Stretch returns briefly to join Noaccount who has not as yet left. He then turns and calls everyone back into the room. He and Noaccount then proceed to lift up the widow Jones, and they put her still unconscious into the box. Stretch motions to everyone to quiet down and they respond sensing the prank. Then he and Noaccount kneel there at the coffin looking directly in on the poor unsuspecting widow. Now even the preacher is in on it. Stretch and Noaccount pretend that they are deeply in prayer. They are there on their knees in exactly the same spot where the widow was praying. Well, she wakes up and sits up, and looks directly into the face of Stretch who is now praying for her. She falls dead away back down into the coffin.

Rags

Barber John is on the side laughing so hard that the tears are falling from his eyes as he holds his stomach.

Rags: Shorty, we'd better go fetch Doc and tell him to come give the widow some salts.

Shorty: Bet she don't go to anymore funerals.

Everyone starts whooping it up as they leave.

Noaccount: Hey, Stretch! *(he yells)* Where you goin?

Stretch: To Heaven…been everywhere else already.

Noaccount: Know who's going to be there at the gate?

Stretch: Who?

Noaccount: The widow Jones.

Chapter 30
A Little Older

We are in the barber shop of Barber John. Barber John is walking back and forth chuckling to himself. Every once in a while he can't restrain himself and he bursts out laughing. With that the door opens and Rags walks in. He has come for his Saturday haircut. He is older now and we can see that time has passed. There is grey in his hair. The man has aged some. He heads right for the barber chair and speaks as he settles down.

Rags: Getting old John.

John is not saying anything but he is trying to hold back the chuckles as he drapes Rags with the apron.

Rags: John…What's so funny?

Barber John: Rags, do you remember when your buddies Stretch and Noaccount down by the tracks got into that discussion about dying? Then they *(laughing out loud now)* held the fake funeral to find out if one of them died if anyone would come?

Rags: Yeah…Noaccount went down and put it into the paper that old Stretch had passed on.

Barber John: Dodds was away and they held the wake right there at the funeral parlor where they worked the very next day. *(now John bursts out in laughter as he tries to start cutting Rags' hair)* The widow, Rags…remember the widow Jones?

Rags: That was funny.

Barber John: (now wiping his eyes as he laughs) Old Stretch popped up and the widow went straight down…*(he can hardly get it out)*…right there in front of the coffin.

Rags is now caught up in the laughing.

Barber John: Everybody was there, the girls from the saloon…the minister…remember the minister….It's a miracle, a miracle!

Rags is really laughing now. As laughter does sometimes, it catches on, and the people doing it lose it, and the laughter becomes self-feeding.

Rags: And old Stretch came back.

Barber John: Yeah, and then he and Noaccount put her in the box. *(John has completely lost it)*

Rags: (wiping his eyes) Then she woke up, saw Stretch and Noaccount praying for her and fell out.

Both men laugh for a while and then just as it started the laughter eases and the mood turns peaceful and reminiscent.

Barber John: (as John gives Rags a haircut) Boy, those were the good old days. Great times.

Rags: Sure were.

Barber John: (after a short while he finishes Rags' haircut) There, that should do it.

John takes a mirror and holds it behind Rags' head so that he can see the haircut he has just received. Rags without acknowledging just slips out of the chair indicating that everything is o.k. As John lowers the mirror they continue talking.

Barber John: What do you have planned for today?

Rags

As Rags reaches into his pocket and retrieves some money to pay John.

Rags: Oh, nothing too much. It's a beautiful day. Thought I'd take a walk over and say hello to Sophia.

Barber John: Boy, how old is that woman anyway?

Rags: John, she's been around since Pikes Peak was a pimple.

Barber John: Well, see you next week Rags.

Rags: (as Rags pays John) Thanks John.

Rags walks out of the shop and into the sunlit street. He breathes deep to take in the fresh air of this beautiful day, then he starts walking toward the side streets of the town.

Chapter 31
Sophia

Rags is walking up to the front outside porch of an older wooden frame house just outside of town. There on the slated wooded deck in the shade is an old, old black lady. Rags ascends the front steps. She is dozing in the cool of the day as she sits in an old rocker. Rags quietly walks over to the rocker and gives the old lady a kiss on the cheek.

Rags: Sophia…*(he whispers...then a little louder)...* Sophia.

The woman opens her eyes and as she does, instantly brings forth a warm smile.

Sophia: Rags…Rags child. Bless my heart.

Rags: Hi, Sophia.

Sophia: Whatever brings you out here on such a beautiful day? You should be playing with the other children.

Rags: Well, as always I just wanted to see my favorite girl. I'm an old man now Sophia. Wish I could go out and play like I used to. My mind says "yes" but my bones say "don't do it fool".

Sophia: (she laughs) If you're old then I got to be ancient. But if you don't tell, I won't tell…hee…hee.

Rags: I just felt like taking a walk and thought that I'd come on out and visit. Is everything alright? Is there anything you need or that I can do for you?

Sophia: Nonsense. You've been doing for me all these years. I know everything ...can't fool an old lady like me. Think I don't know who's been watching out for me all these years. Just 'cause I never said thank you, don't mean I don't know.

Rags: Sophia you've said thank you so many times in so many ways. You just been a good part of my life.

Sophia: Well, I'm sure glad that I don't have to still change your diapers. How would you like some cold water...or tea?

Rags: Some cold water would be real nice. Don't you bother though, I'll get it from the well.

Sophia: No you won't neither. Mary...*(she calls out toward the door)*...Daughter...

She waits a moment and then there is a reply. The voice of Mary gets louder as she approaches the door.

Mary: Mama? *(she steps out and sees Rags)* Hi, Rags ... How are you?

Rags: Mary, how are you?

Mary: Oh just fine.

Sophia: Daughter, bring Rags some 'that cool water, chill him down.

Rags: And the boys? And Moses?

Mary: Everyone is just fine, thank you, Rags. I'll get you some water. Sit, relax awhile.

Rags: Thanks Mary the walk out made me a little thirsty.

Mary goes inside and Rags sits down. By the time he sits she is back and hands him a glass of water.

Rags: Thank you. *(he drinks the water)* Boy that's nice and cold.

Mary: Let me get you some more.

Rags: No thank you, Mary. That was just fine.

Mary: Rags, please excuse me but I'm in the kitchen making supper. Why don't you stay and have supper with us?

Rags: That's very thoughtful Mary but I want to be heading back soon. Thank you for asking me. It's hard to turn down your good cooking. Can I accept the offer for another time?

Mary: You know you can. There ain't no time you won't be welcomed here.

Rags: Thanke' Marr....

Mary then returns to the kitchen and Rags looks over at Sophia. She has almost dozed off during his conversation with Mary. Rags smiles.

Rags: Sophia, I think I'll be heading back. *(he raises himself and stretches)*

The scene shifts to the back of the medium wood frame house. Behind the house are fields and a small vegetable garden. The house although not a shambles, is not as well kept as it might be. Aside from the large open front porch that we have seen there is a smaller screened in back porch. An old black gent wearing a large straw hat and coveralls is leisurely and carefully caring for the garden. There is a wooded area directly behind the fields and coming out of that wooded area is a path which goes directly beside the garden. Walking down that path through the straw colored fields are two young black working age men. Each is carrying a fishing pole. They are happily talking as they go. Now they are approaching the garden. As they come abreast of the old man working there, the outermost of the two fellows holds up two very large catfish and turns toward the man.

First Fellow: Hi, Moses.

Second Fellow: Hey Moses, Mama's gonna be happy tonight. *(gesturing toward the catch)*

Moses: Mighty fine looking catch. *(shakes his head; takes a handkerchief from his back pocket and wipes his brow)*

Both boys smile as they hurry up the back steps of the old house. The back screen door swings open as the two with an air of excitement enter.

First Fellow: Mama,… hey mama, look here.

As the first fellow enters the kitchen, the second fellow takes both fishing poles and places them in the corner of the porch. As we enter the kitchen we see Mary, who is obviously the mother of the boys. She is working over the sink which has an outside pump, inside. She is pushing on the handle drawing water.

Mary: Well gracious me. Look what we have here. Looks like we gonna have us some good deep fry tonight.

The boys lay the fish in the sink and each in turn gives her a hug.

Second Fellow: Where's grandma, mama?

Mary: Out on the porch. *(gesturing to the front of the house)* I guess I'm elected to clean the catch of the day.

The two boys go through the front door.

First Fellow: Grams, you must of been praying for us 'cause we had some good luck today.

We can see Rags off in the distance. He has left and is returning home. The boys can see him also.

Sophia: God provides.

Second Fellow: 'Specially if you use the right bait. *(referring to the fish)*

Sophia: Watch your words. Sometimes they bites harder than the mouth they comes out of. You best remember what I tell you…God provides. *(looking towards Rags as he walks away)*

First Fellow: Yeah, you must be right grandma. Like for that fella Rags there. *(he gestures toward Rags who is off in the distance now)* We see him in the park in town all the time. Boy he don't ever seem to do nothin'.

Second Fellow: And don't ever seem to need nothin' either. *(looking toward the other fellow)* How's he do that? Must be some kind of miracle.

Sophia: Miracle? *(with a slight laugh)* If your eyes could only see what these old eyes have seen. That easy life wasn't always so easy. There's a heavy price been paid. Your old granny knows. Best you mind your tongue and your ways; you treat that man Rags right.

With that the door opens and a voice is heard. It's Mary addressing the two young men.

Mary: Thomas, go out back now and fetch your grandpa. Roy, you come in here and help your mother get ready for dinner, after you wash up. *(gesturing at them)* Mama's dinner be ready in a little bit.

Sophia: Let me come in and help child.

Mary: Mama you just sit now. There's nothing in here to do that needs doing, it's already been done. Roy, into the house with you. Tell Moses to give you some tomatoes. *(her voice fades)* Tell him to come on in and get ready. We'll be eating soon.

Everyone has now entered the house except Sophia. Now alone she speaks to herself.

Sophia: A heavy price.

The scene now draws in on Rags who is paused at the side of the road. Leaning up against, and with his foot raised and resting on the lowest rail of the split rail fence, Rags gazes out over the field fresh with apple blossoms and apple trees which just now begin to silhouette against the reddened sky of the oncoming evening. Rags lowers himself and bends now scooting through the opening between the rails of the fence. Straightening up on the opposite side he begins to wander toward the apple trees in the small orchard. He approaches one of the trees and moves close to it. Gently he raises his hand palm outward and rests it against the tree as if to feel its heart beat. Closing his eyes he breathes in deep. There is a cluster of blossoms near Rags' face. He takes in the aroma of the apple blossoms with his breath. We can see his face now deep in the memory of a fragrance of a time past. The face begins to change. It is a young Rags, a boy in exactly the same position with his hand up against the tree and now with a slight smile on his face taking in the wonder of the smell of the apple blossoms. His eyes closed and lost in the moment, suddenly his eyes open, as he hears the voice of his Grandmother Sara calling to him.

(The flashback is to Rags in his youth. He is living with his grandparents, Joshua and Sara.)

Sara: Rags…Oh Rags…Come in now son, it's getting dark.

The young Rags leaves the tree and scoots toward the house. There he is met by Sara at the door. She hugs him and ushers him into the house, speaking to him as they enter.

Sara: Playing out by the trees were you.

Rags: Yes, ma'am.

Sara: I know it's a real special treat this time of year. Pretty soon these flowers will turn into apples. And then those apples will turn into grandma's pies. *(Rags smiles in response to the pies)* Now off with you…get washed and ready for bed.

Joshua has been taking this all in, as he sits by the open window, looking out and meditating on the moment. Rags disappears from the scene now leaving Sara and Joshua alone. Without taking his eyes from the window he speaks to his wife.

Joshua: Sara, can you remember back to when we first met. Funny how just now everything is as clear to me as it was then.

Sara: I can Joshua. In fact when I smell the blossoms this time of year it takes me all the way back so that sometimes I can still smell the sweet fragrance of the apple blossoms in front of the residence house where I lived as a little girl. It was a wonderful time Joshua… A wonderful time…

Joshua: Yes, Sara. I remember everything so clearly today for some reason. I remember how on that following day I went up to see Elder Harris. How kind and warm he was. How he welcomed me and told me I could stay with the family for as long as I wanted and that I would be a brethren for as long as I wished. He explained to me that day about how God gave all of us free will and how they tried to live according to God's will which is His word, which is Christ Jesus. I guess I just didn't understand much about it then, but the love and the peace of these fine people, it was incredible. I remember coming down from that meeting and instead of putting me right to work, there was Smitty and Eddie waiting for me with fishing poles in hand. We went down to the pond that day and fished and swam all day long. Smitty, I remember him well. I loved him as a boy; and big as he was he was gentle as a mouse. There were so many good people there Sara; Joseph in the print shop; and do you remember Mark at the timber mill...and, and brother Jason in the machine shop....It was quite a group, wasn't it Sara?

(All of the time Joshua is speaking we see these scenes from the Shaker village.)

Joshua: *(continues)* You know Sara, in Sunday service I could never take my eyes off of you. You were the most beautiful thing I think I'd ever seen. *(laughing)*...You were even more beautiful than some of the horses Smitty showed me. Do you remember when I told you that?

Sara: Yes...I hit you with a pillow.

They both laugh.

Joshua: *(continues)* I loved to watch you sing and dance in service. And you looked nice in your blue and white Sunday dress. The time, Sara... The time... where did the time go?

Sara: I know Josh....I know. And I remember the most important decision of my life. It was when you decided that you wanted to go out into the world and start out on your own. The thought of you leaving, well, I thought that the world had just fallen out from under me. You asked me to leave with you, but as always, explained that I had free will and the right to choose whichever way of life I wanted. Secretly, I had always dreamed of having a family of my own that I could bring up just as I had been brought up in my Shaker family of believers; surrounded by love, and peace, and good works. And with you leaving, the thought of never being able to have those things was heavy on my heart. And above all, God knows each person's heart. And my heart was as easy for him to read as an open book. To deny you and me together would have made me very unhappy and I know God in all of his love wants his children to be happy. That Sunday in church when I knew that you were leaving, well, I just couldn't help myself, my love for you was too strong. I had to go with you.

We now see a repeat of the exact same scene we saw when they were young, of Sara running across the field after leaving the church to join Joshua as he finishes loading the wagon before they leave the Shaker village. However this time we see it from a window in the room of Elder Harris on the upper floor of the meeting hall, where Eddie first took Joshua to meet him. Neither Josh, nor Sara, ever realized that the Elder Harris had known their feelings all along and had seen the entire departure develop. As he looks down on them from the window the Elder speaks.

Elder Harris: May God hold you both to his bosom, bless you with his many blessings, and shield you with his love all the days of your life. God bless and welcome home.

Joshua: They were wonderful days Sara, full of blessings. I guess it was just God's way of bringing you to me, and me to you. I thank Him for that.

Sara: But life is not all roses. I love you Joshua J. Jenkins, I do. And for all we've been through to this day, I give thanks for the roses and never curse the thorns.

Joshua: Sara, I'm very tired. I love you. *(quietly, half to himself)* ...Mama I love you,... Papa I love you.

The scene fades forward again to Rags who is still at the apple tree in the field not far from Sophia's house. The sun has not yet fully set. We can see the face of Rags. There are tears streaming down the cheeks of the burly old coot. He takes a deep breath, pats the trunk of the tree and wipes his eyes dry. Then turning he returns to the fence and crouches under the rail, letting himself out once again onto the road and back into the present. As he starts to walk we can hear the sound of a

Rags

wagon coming closer. It is the boys from Sophia's house. They stop next to Rags.

Boys: Mr. Rags. It's getting dark. Can we give you a lift to town? We're going that way.

Rags: Thank you, boys. That's mighty kind of you.

With this Rags jumps on board and they drive off on the road toward town.

Chapter 32
The Aunt

The scene opens and we see Billy outside in his back yard. He is a little older now, about junior high school age and there in the brightness of the mid-morning sun he struggles to chop some wood. Behind him stands a large pile of evenly stacked cut wood quarters. There on an old stump Billy struggles to split some log sections with an axe in front of the already huge pile of split logs. As the young boy chops away we hear the call of two young voices. We see a young boy and a young girl. The girl and boy are longtime friends of Billy and as he looks up, an obvious look of happiness comes over his face. The girl is called Jenny and the boy is Chinese, complete with pigtail and kimono. They both approach Billy. The Chinese boy with his arms crossed and his hands in the oversized sleeves of his kimono, bows.

Chop Chop: Hi, Billy.

The little girl just looks on.

Billy: Hi, Chop Chop! Hi, Jenny!

Jenny: Come on Billy. Let's go down to the wharf.

Billy: (with reluctance as he looks at the stack of wood, and the wood still left to chop) Sure would like to…but…well, you know. My aunt says that I have to do my chores.

Chop Chop: We'll help you, Billy. Then we can go down to the wharf. The boats are coming in today.

Billy: Really!

Jenny: Yes…What's that? *(pointing to an old broken rain barrel)*

Billy: Oh, just an old rain barrel I have to chop up for firewood.

Chop Chop: Great! Let's chop it up now. Then we can use the metal rings to roll.

Jenny: Yeah!

Billy: O.k.

So the three, given way to the fashion of children, start to disassemble the old rain barrel. In no time at all the slats are separated from the old brown rusted rings that for so many years have held it together. As the slats and rings are laid on the ground Chop Chop bends over and retrieves the fallen iron rings. Keeping the largest one for himself he hands the next largest one to Billy and the smallest one to Jenny. Jenny looking and comparing the rings speaks. In a somewhat resentful and sharp tone she relates her feelings even though there is a slight question in her voice.

Jenny: How come I got the littlest one?

Billy: Because you're a girl.

Jenny: That's not fair.

Chop Chop: There's an old Chinese proverb that says even the smallest ring is just as round.

Everyone looks at Chop Chop.

Billy: Wow, Chop Chop! O.k.! How old is that Chinese saying?

Chop Chop: About two minutes old now. There is another also which says, *(pointing his finger into the air as if to speak with authority)*…"Man who cannot make up old Chinese proverb instantly ends up with the smallest ring".

Billy and Chop Chop start laughing.

Jenny: That's not fair. You guys are awful.

Then without hesitation she grabs a stick and hitting the upright ring in front of her starts to roll it out of the yard running after it as she goes.

Jenny: Last one to the wharf is a rotten egg.

Just as Jenny utters her challenge there comes a sharp and nasty voice from the house. It is Billy's aunt.

Billy: (toward Chop Chop) Quick, hide… There behind the wood pile.

Chop Chop without hesitation scampers behind the wood pile just as the aunt appears out of the back door. Approaching Billy, she speaks in a sharp and commanding voice.

Aunt: Boy, you chop that wood…and then you get inside and clean that house. Best you start supper for me so when I return I don't have to be bothered cooking. When your mother left you with me she left me with just one more burden. Least you can do is make my life easier. I'll be going downtown with that nice salesman gentleman who comes to town from time to time. *(She is all dressed up with parasol to match. Then lifting her nose into the air and turning to leave)*…fix your own supper and don't wait up for me.

With that she turns toward the front of the yard, turns left and starts to walk toward the town.

Chop Chop: (peeking out from behind the woodpile) Phew… that was close. Is she gone?

Billy: Yes…*(saddened).* She's gone.

Chop Chop: Old Chinese proverb says, "If old lady look behind big wood pile, sees little Chinese boy wet his kimono"… Let's go Billy, we have to catch Jenny or we'll be rotten eggs.

Billy: Yeah, let's go get her.

Both boys then grabbing sticks start rolling their iron rings in front of them as they roll themselves out of the yard in the same direction that Jenny went and in the opposite direction that the aunt went.

Soon they are at the wharf. We see the three children approaching, rolling their rings in front of them, almost in a dead heat. Jenny is momentarily exhausted as she comes to a halt and the ring drops. All three pause to look out over the inlet that leads to the bay and then to the ocean. There the three sit on the ends of the pilings which anchor the wharf to the ocean floor.

Chop Chop: You know my father didn't always own a laundry. Once he lived in a place called Shanghai.

Billy: What did he do there Chop Chop?

Chop Chop: He worked in a tavern on a wharf just like this one. Just like in that tavern over there, that old sailors bar that has been abandoned. In fact I'll bet that that place is just like the one my father used to work in. He used to tell me about how they used to hijack sailors for voyages far across the sea.

Billy: Shanghai sailors!

Jenny: Really?

Chop Chop: Yes, really. There was a trap door in the floor of the bar. And when the sailor would get drunk enough they would open the secret door and they would fall below to a small boat. Then they would be taken to a large boat and they would be out to sea before they woke up sober enough to ever know the difference.

Billy: Wow!

Chop Chop: Now would you like to see my secret?

Jenny: Secret?

Billy: Yes. What secret Chop Chop?

They go inside the old abandoned bar. The two boys and Jenny are at the edge of a cut out in the floor looking at the sea water below. It is a trap door just like the one Chop Chop has described to the others. They look at each other in amazement with their eyes widened by the experience.

Chop Chop: (as they pull the trap door back up) Swear an oath that you will never tell anyone about the secret door I have found and showed you. *(the trap door is now in place)*

Billy: I swear.

Chop Chop and Billy: Jenny.

Jenny: Oh well, o.k. ... I swear.

Chop Chop: Good.

Billy: Can I try it once?

Jenny: Yeah...me too.

Chop Chop: Well, o.k....just once.

With that both Billy and Jenny race to the old bar. There behind the bar amongst the cobwebs and abandoned dusty bottles and glasses is a wooden lever. The two of them together pull the lever and we hear the trap door fall.

Jenny: Oh Neat!

Both Jenny and Billy jump up and down as if they have accomplished something of great relevance. Then the three leave through the front door of the old abandoned bar.

Billy: Well, I guess I'd better get back to the house and do my chores.

Jenny: O.k. Billy. See you tomorrow.

Chop Chop: Remember, it's a secret. Don't tell anyone.

Billy: I won't.

As he says this he departs to the right, and the others go on their way in the opposite direction toward the water.

Billy starts back and after a short time pauses to look back upon his two friends as they walk down near the water skimming stones and shells across the top of the water. Then looking down at his dog Boxcar who has been with him throughout this entire episode, he explains.

Billy: Boxcar, I sure wish we could stay and play some more, but we'd better get back before Aunt Eveler gets back. She gets so mad all of the time. Boxcar, why did mama have to get so sick? We have to go visit mama soon, again. *(the dog wags his tail)*

Soon we are in front of the big old house where Billy lives. He has finally gotten back and is approaching the front door. He opens the front door now to enter. Immediately upon entering the house and before the door even closes we hear the crack of a whip. Billy screams out in astonishment and pain.

Aunt: You ungrateful wretch!! You're just like your mother. This is what my step sister left me with… You!... An ungrateful, sniveling wretch who does not obey his elders. *(with this she lashes out once again at him)*…No wonder your mother is in the crazy house, with all those loonies… And you're just like her!

Billy: My mom is sick…She's not crazy, she's not. The doctor says she will get better.

Aunt: That'll be the day…Huh…*(mockingly, then yelling at him)* Did you finish your chores?!!

Rags

Billy: (as he cringes) I finished all the chopping, honest I did. Please don't hit me anymore. *(he breaks down and starts crying)*

Aunt: Sniveling brat! It's bad enough that that self-satisfying salesman didn't show up, but on top of that I have to come home and find you out sneaking around, probably with your heathen slant eyed yellow friend. Soon your eyes will look just like that if you keep hanging around with him…Oh well, where's my dinner? You were supposed to get it ready.

Just then there is a knock on the door. She grabs the boy and pulls him out of the way by his arm. Placing the willow whip behind the door so that whoever is entering cannot see it she opens the door. It is the salesman. Instantly her poison personality changes and turns to sugar.

Aunt: Oh…*(with surprise)*…Do please come in. Billy and I were just discussing you and what a fine gentleman you are. I was telling Billy how much I would like him to grow up to be just like you. Oh, dear, here…let me take your jacket. I was just about to make some supper, and you're just in time to join us.

Harry: Thank you, Eveler. You sure are one lucky boy, Billy, to have such a good aunt.

Billy: Yes, sir. *(with this Billy and Boxcar go off toward his room)* Boxcar, remind me when I grow up not to become a salesman. And, if I do, remind me not to visit anybody's aunt.

The scene shifts to the salesman and the aunt as they talk in the living room of the old house. Billy instead of going to his room has stopped and has seated himself with his faithful friend and companion Boxcar, at the head of the stairs. Saddened he overhears all that is to be said between the two of them.

Harry: Well, Eveler, let me come right to the point. You

know I've been a salesman for a long time now and well some things can't change, and my being a salesman is one of them.

Aunt: Oh Harry you are so to the point and such a good salesman.

Harry: That being the point, Eveler. I've made up my mind about what we were discussing last time I was in town. I do want to marry you.

Aunt: Oh Harry, you darling man. I love you too, Harry. And as I was saying to Billy, it would be my most fondest dream come true if only Harry Olsmer would take me as his wife.

Harry: However, Eveler, we are not without a major problem.

Aunt: There is no problem too great for love, Harry.

Harry: Well, Eveler…you see…I'm a traveling salesman and I can't change that. However, if I get married I would want my wife to be with me. That means a great deal of traveling and moving around. Now with Billy that would be quite a problem. I couldn't take the three of us everywhere.

Aunt: Oh Harry, dearest Harry. That will be no problem. You see this is my sister-in-law's house. It actually belongs to Billy. I'll just find someone to look after him here until we settle down. Then we'll come back and get him. Oh, we will be sure to check in on him and make sure everything is always alright. His mother is in an institution you know.

Harry: You're such a good lady, Eveler. Do you think it would work? I mean have you someone who will look after the boy?

Aunt: Definitely…Don't give it a second thought. Just think Harry,…me and you… our honeymoon…Oh Harry.

Billy: Well Boxcar, I think we just got our walking papers. I think he bought it …hook, line and sinker.

Harry: Shall I talk to Billy?

Aunt: No Harry, it will be better if I tell him about the wonderful news. We have such a wonderful understanding.

With this the aunt starts toward the stairs. Hearing her coming, Billy and Boxcar scamper to his room. As she climbs the stairs she is talking to herself.

Aunt: I'll find someone to look after him if it's the last thing on earth that I do. He'll not stop me from having a life. My good sister had her life and now it's time for me and I'm not going to have her little 'Billy boy' be the reason I don't.

Aunt: Oh Billy…*(in a loud and sweet voice intended for the man who is waiting downstairs to hear)*… I have such wonderful news.

Then turning her head back in the direction in which she is walking and away from the stairs, she enters Billy's room. The dog snarls at her.

Billy: Easy Boxcar.

Aunt: Stay in this room with that four legged flea hotel and don't let me hear one word from you or it's the whip for both of you.

She exits the room as fast as she entered it shutting the door behind her. As she descends the stairs we can hear her speaking to the salesman in her "oh too velvet" voice.

Aunt: …Oh, he's so thrilled…He congratulated us. We've made him so happy.

With this the scene fades.

Chapter 33
The Institution

The next scene opens with Billy at his mother's side within the dingy grey walls of the prison-like mental institution. Tears are running down his cheeks as he is speaking to her. Then fighting back his real emotions he fakes a smile. His mother just stares straight ahead and as Billy speaks to her she shows absolutely no response.

Billy: Mom, I'll be back to see you real soon. I'd better start back now. Everything is fine at home. Don't you worry, mom. Just get better...'Bye mom...

Billy leans over to give his mother a kiss. She just continues to stare.

The scene gets greyer and darker until the scene fades.

Chapter 34
Barber Shop News

When the light comes up again, we are once again in the barber shop. John is removing a hot towel from Rags' face.

Rags: Feels real good, John.

Barber John: (now wiping Rags' face with a towel) There you go Rags…How's that?

Rags: I look forward to these towels, John, especially in the winter. Feels real good…fabulous. Hey John, speaking about winter, does that young fellow Billy still work for you?

Barber John: Funny you should mention him, Rags. He just came in here the other day and asked if I could use him. You know Rags, I've been thinking, *(pause)*… maybe I should take him in as an apprentice and teach him the Barber trade. It ain't much, but it's honest, and seeing how he's come on some pretty hard times.

Rags: (now getting up out of his chair and brushing himself off) What do you mean, hard times?

Barber John: Well it seems his mom took ill. Mental you know. In the institution for the crazy as I understand it. The boy was living with his aunt, and she flew the coop with a traveling salesman. *(pause)* Remember when you saved his puppy? Full grown now…calls him Boxcar, ya know.

Rags: You don't say… Sorry to hear that…real sorry.

Rags

Barber John: Looks like he's heading for some big trouble himself. Kid hangs out with that bunch downtown. That's how it begins.

Rags: Is that right, John. Hmmm…Still live in the big old grey house?

Barber John: Sure does.

Rags: Hmmm…

Barber John: If someone doesn't do something real soon he's going to come to no good.

Rags: How old is the boy now, John?

Barber John: School age. He's older now… you know time isn't waiting for you, or me, or anyone.

Rags pops on his derby hat and puts a cigar into his mouth. Then after lighting it hands John some money and leaves. As he leaves we can detect the concerned concentration of his thinking by the wrinkled brow and stern look on his face.

Chapter 35
Hooch

Looking up from the ground we see the trunk of a "Long Bean" tree. Against the backdrop of sky and branches we see Billy climbing higher and higher pulling the long pods off of the branches as he goes. From below we hear the encouragement and cheers of his fellow gang members.

Gang: Atta boy, Billy. Get me some good ones. Hey Billy, get that one to your right, it's a real winner.

Billy makes a long reach and retrieves the pod to his right. Then, transferring it to the other hand he slides down the tree and jumps to the ground.

Gang: Gimme one, Billy.

Billy: Alright there's enough for everyone. Here... *(handing out the long and slender pods)*

Gang: Who has matches?

Billy: Me, who else.

Gang: Alright! Bil...lee! Let's light up.

Then as each holds the pod in their mouth, as in the fashion of a cigarette, Billy goes around and lights them while they puff to get them started. Then the gang sits down beneath the tree and they continue to smoke their poor man's cigarettes.

Gang: **Anyone got the "Hooch"?** *(everyone laughs as one boy holds up the bottle)* **Yeah, Jimmy. Pass that bottle brother.**

The boys continue smoking, laughing and drinking.

Chapter 36
Rags Visits Billy

The scene cuts to the big old house where Billy lives. There we see Rags ascending the front porch steps. The yard around the house is overgrown and unattended. He approaches the front door and then after a moment of waiting pushes at the front door as he knocks. The door having been left unlatched swings slightly open from the slight force of the knocks. Rags slowly and gently pushes the door further, opening it more, and carefully walks in. Cautiously he calls.

Rags: Billy………Billy, you in here?

No one answers as Rags continues to call. He waits and then enters further into the house, shocked to see that the house that he once visited, that was so warm and clean was now strewn with old clothes, dirty dishes and the like. Slowly Rags looks around the dust laden room and sees the disarray which now surrounds him. For a moment he stands with his hands on his hips. Removing the cigar from his lips he begins to shake his head in disbelief. He raises his cigar as if lost as to where to flick the ashes, and then shrugging his shoulders, he just flicks the ashes onto the floor. This he does in a manner as if to say, "Oh, what the hell's the difference it's so dirty anyway".

Suddenly we hear someone approaching up the outer steps of the house. "Oops!!" We hear the person miss a step. Now we can see through the open door just a bit. It's Billy. He staggers through the door at first without noticing Rags. Too woozy to be startled to any great degree he stops and stares for a moment when he notices Rags standing there.

Rags: Billy?

Billy does not answer. He just keeps coming closer as if trying to get a better look.

Rags: (again) Patches? Is that you Patches?

Billy: (in a ragged unsure voice) Rags? Rags…is that you?

Rags: I sure hope so. If it ain't, I got a lot of explaining to do to a lot of people. Of course it's me! *(pauses)* Boy, have you grown up.

Billy moves over to an easy chair and falls into it.

Billy: I feel a little dizzy.

Then without warning he bolts up, covering his mouth at the same time, and makes a B-line for the bathroom where we can see his back bent over the toilet and we hear him vomiting.

Rags walks over in a cool way and leans on the frame of the doorway looking in on him.

Rags: What you been doing, boy? Drinking? Smoking? *(Billy raises himself enough to face Rags)* If you have boy, you got to pay the price. Remember this son …there ain't no pleasure if there ain't no pain. And from the looks of you, there sure was a lot of pleasure, 'cause you're a wreck.

With this in a real cool manner Rags blows smoke into the face of Billy. The smell of the smoke only makes Billy start in vomiting all the more, all over again.

Rags: Sorry 'bout that.

Billy: (after he finally pulls himself together enough to speak, he mumbles) Thanks a lot.

Rags

Rags: Put some cold water on your face and come out here. I can see we have some heavy duty talking to do young fella.

Rags then moves away into the messy kitchen. We can hear the water as Billy washes his face. Soon Billy enters the kitchen also. Towel in hand he dries his face.

Rags: Well now...That's better. Boy, have you eaten anything?

Billy: (putting both hands on the sides of his head) I ain't hungry.

Rags: Don't you know that ain't, ain't right. What do they teach you in that school?

Billy: School...ha...What good's school anyway?

Rags just looks and starts to pause a bit.

Rags: Hmmm...I understand that your mother's not feeling too well.

Billy: Yes...Ma's ill. But she'll get better.

Rags: Yes, she will. Who is here to take care of you now?

Billy: Me...I can take care of myself. Eveler used to take care of me, but no more. She was my aunt, but she said I was like Ma. She was a mean old lady. I tried so hard but it didn't seem to matter. No matter what I did it never seemed to be enough. I tried so hard to love her...She was so mean to me. Finally went off with a salesman 'bout a year or so ago.

Rags: Without you obviously.

Billy: Yeah, without me. Thank God!

Rags: (laughing) Where'd they go?

Billy: On some kind of honeymoon cruise...I think.

Rags: Honeymoon?

Rags

Billy: Yes. They were going on some new ship called the Titanic.

Rags: Well, I guess she deserved it.

Billy: Guess so...

Rags: How do you manage here alone.

Billy: Well, I work odd jobs. Sometimes the guys help me out.

Rags: So I hear.

Billy: Yes, they're my friends.

Rags: I guess that's what friends are for, to help if they can.

Billy: It will be easier this year. Think I'll quit school and go to work.

Rags: I see. And quitting school will be a step in making your life better? Well, that would be your second mistake.

Billy: My second mistake? What was my first?

Rags: Not knowing who your best friend in the whole world is.

Billy: Who's that?

Rags: You'll see. But I'll tell you right now, you are better off finishing school. You may really need it in the world that's shaping up ahead of you. Once you start quitting you may never stop.

Billy who was sitting in a chair near the table has completely fallen asleep with his head on the table.

Rags: Wow, I really impressed him. Oh well, I'll be back.

The scene fades.

Chapter 37
Cow Tipping

The evening is crisp and clear and the stars light up the blue-black sky like a string of Christmas lights strung out around the bulb called the moon. In the still of the night the chirping of crickets and of frogs can be heard. A dim light emits from the still half opened door of the old grey house of Billy. A group of kids gathers and approaches the house. It is the group that Billy hangs out with. They call him.

Gang: Hey Billy, come on out. Billy, Bil,,,lee

Bllly comes to the door wiping the drowsiness from his eyes.

Billy: (*spoken with excitement*) Hey guys…Where are you off to?

Gang: Come on Billy. Let's go tip over some of Farmer Shepherd's cows.

Billy: What about school tomorrow?

Gang: Aww…forget school, let's have some fun. There's a lot of cows out there needs tipping, Billy.

It is later that same night and we find the gang, including Billy, sneaking up on cows that are asleep in Farmer Shepherd's pasture. Some cows are asleep on their feet. The boys sneak up to the cow and tip it over. They venture closer and closer to the old red barn in their folly, tipping as they go. But then just as

Rags

they are about to tip one cow near the barn, the constable who was hiding in wait for them pounces out and seizes one of the boys. Naturally the boy that he seizes is Billy.

Constable Red: Got you, you little hoodlum.

Farmer Shepherd: Atta' boy Red, hold'em, I'll help you. *(helping Red)* There you wise guy. I knew you would be out again, but this time we were ready for you.

Constable Red: Well look at who we have here. Seems you're making a full time job out of getting into trouble, ah boy. Makes no never mind 'cause you're going to jail.

Billy: Oh shit!

Farmer Shepherd: 'Bout time we caught up with you guys. Breaking equipment…abusing animals…stealing food.

Billy: I didn't break no equipment. And I sure didn't steal your damn food.

Constable Red: (shaking the boy by his shoulders) Watch your mouth, son. You're in enough trouble already.

Farmer Shepherd: Who were those others that ran away and left you to take all the blame and punishment?

Billy: No one… I don't know.

Constable Red: Well, maybe you will feel better talking to the judge. Come on we're going to town, right now.

Chapter 38
The Trial

They take Billy to the small town hall which acts as the town's courtroom also. There in front of the judge, an older man wearing a plaid shirt, suspenders and specs, stands Constable Red, Farmer Shepherd and Billy.

The back door to the room opens. Quietly walking through the door and taking a seat unnoticed by all is the one man who knows every move that is being made in "his town", Rags.

Judge: Consider this here court in session, and tell me what the hell is going on here.

Constable Red: Judge, the others got away but I got this one. There we were, Farmer Shepherd and me, waiting in the pitch black night just like we planned. We knew they'd be back. Oh we been planning this Judge, yes we have. We've been waiting many a night to get'em and we finally did. Yes sir're Judge, we did. See I waited there behind the old barn door. It were cool and dark but that didn't bother me none at all. I just waited like a good officer of the law should, didn't matter how adverse the conditions, no sir, I didn't mind. Just wanted to uphold the law you know. Well I…

At this point Farmer Shepherd nudges Constable Red and we hear him tell Red in a slightly irritated tone.

Farmer Shepherd: Red, tell him about me too, not just what you did.

Constable Red: (clearing his throat) Ahem...Actually Farmer Shepherd here did help me Judge. See after I apprehended this here violent criminal he had to help me hold him so'in he would not get away...Well, like I was saying it were cold and dark when I, at great risk to myself, pounced out and grabbed this here one.

The Judge at this point nearly completely out of patience waiting to hear something of the facts, blurts out.

Judge: Oh come on for Pete's sake, will somebody tell me what the hell is going on here. The facts...any facts, please.

Constable Red: (clearing his throat) Ahem...Yes sir. They's been tipping over Farmer Shepherd's cows sir, been harassing the good Farmer and his livestock and been abusing public property.

Farmer Shepherd: These vandals been harassing me for the longest time and tipping my cows ain't the worst of it. Been stealing my eggs. Once they even tied the tails of my two donkeys together. Damn near kicked themselves to death I tell you.

The Judge turns his face so as not to let the boy see him laugh, then turns with a serious face and while pulling on both suspenders with his thumbs speaks.

Judge: Young man, what do you have to say?

Billy: We were just having some fun your honor. *(his voice is very nervous)* We didn't mean no harm.

Judge: Fun you call it. Who were the other boys with you?

Billy: Just some of my friends your honor.

Judge: (continues) I asked you a question, boy.

Billy does not answer.

Judge: I see. Lost your tongue. Well, maybe a night in the "hoosegow" will jog that memory of yours.

Then just as the Judge raises his gavel to strike it and pass sentence a voice cuts across the room from the back.

Rags: (real slow and respectful) Your honor. Can I speak with you for a minute?

Judge: Sure Rags, what is it?

Rags walks up toward the Judges table. The Judge rises. When he does, both the Constable and Farmer Shepherd spring up to attention like two jerks. The Judge just motions them to be seated with his hand. Rags walks over to him. He puts his arm around the Judges shoulder as they walk away toward the window. The window is open and both men stand in front of it chatting. From time to time we can hear the Judge say to Rags.

Judge: Is that so…Hmmm…that so… Is that so….?

Then Rags goes back to his seat and the Judge goes back to his table.

Judge: Because of the extenuating circumstances involved in the case …

He is interrupted by the Constable speaking to the good Farmer.

Constable Red: See extenuating, extenuating, I told you.

Farmer Shepherd: (cheering) Give it to 'em Judge.

Judge: Look, Sherlock and Watson, if you don't mind. *(continues)* Because of the extenuating circumstances involved here, and because I know Rags here, my judgment is as follows: I Theodore Judd the third, by the power vested in me here in the good state of Massachusetts do hereby remit this here young whippersnapper to the recognizance of my friend Rags.

(to Billy) Boy so you fully understand that means in everyday language, "You better listen to him, or else". If I ever see you again in this here courtroom, I'm gonna have you hanged. *(to Rags)* Rags, take care of this delinquent…Case closed.

Billy and Rags leave the court. There in the front of the room is the Judge, the Constable, and Farmer Shepherd all shaking hands and laughing and congratulating each other.

Judge: You guys nearly cracked me up. Red, when you started carrying on, and on, and on 'bout how you waited in the cold, dark night, I nearly wet my socks.

Red: Teddy you even had me fooled. You know you would make a real good judge, honest. *(they all laugh)*

Farmer Shepherd: You guys are both "Hams". Both of you belong on Broadway. Now me, I think I'll just go out there to Cal-i-for-nia to that Hollywood place.

Red: Boy, that Rags sure knows how to do things. When he wants something done it sure gets done, doesn't it.

Judge: He really wanted to straighten out this kid. Said something about a promise that he made when the boy was real young.

Red: Well, if'in he turns out anything like Rags he'll be alright. And he'll have a heck of a time getting alright.

The three continue talking and laughing as the scene changes to Billy and Rags outside the town hall.

Rags walks up to Billy in an understanding way, he puts his arm out, shakes his hand, and musses up his hair.

Rags: Come on. Let's get you home and start sorting out your life. Looks like it's gonna be a new life for you, old buddy. Just Patches and Rags; Rags and Patches from now on…Is that o.k.? *(says Rags looking down at him, as would a father to a son)*

Billy: (pause) …that's o.k… *(says Billy with a slight and happy smile)*

Billy has finally found a friend who is willing to go to bat for him.

They continue to walk down the street together as the sun fades into the warm evening air.

They will start their new journey together.

Authors Message

And that's not the end of our story. You see Rags did rescue Patches, and did guide him clear of the bad elements in life. He taught him what was important in life; goodness and the values Joshua had learned from the Shaker Village, hard work, simplicity, appreciating accomplishing goals, and making things that help make other people's lives better.

Rags may have thought he had a full life. He had seen a lot, and done many things, and figured maybe that was all. But you have to be careful sometimes, because just when you think it's over, life sometimes throws you a curve ball (or a cabbage ball). Someone comes into your life, or something happens that changes everything and turns your world upside down. This can be easy change, or not so easy change, but it's always change, and that's usually for the better. For Rags it will come in the form of a small boy, who he promised to watch out for named Patches. What will happen, what that change will be, who knows, but that's for another story.

For now we have Rags, and a beautiful story of love, life and happiness.

We hope people who read this story can take something good from it, from the good value lives of Joshua and Sara, to the new responsibilities of Rags for Patches. We believe most people are good people, and hope it stays that way, and as Patches found out with Rags, sometimes you don't have to find them, good people will find, and help you.

And that's our story, a story of love, life and happiness and as the Elder Harris would say, "May God hold you to his bosom, bless you with his many blessings, and shield you with his love all the days of your life. God bless and welcome home."

About the Author

Joseph Durante was born above his grandfather's barber shop in Hackensack, New Jersey. He received his Bachelor of Science degree from Rutgers University College of Agriculture and his Doctor of Dental Surgery from Fairleigh Dickenson University.

Louis Durante graduated from Holy Cross College in Massachusetts and the Webber Douglas School of Drama in England. He also studied at the Royal Academy of Dramatic Art in England.

f9+8ThTc